sex kittens and
dawgs fall in

maryrose wood

sex kittens and horn dawgs fall in love

delacorte press

Published by Delacorte Press
an imprint of Random House Children's Books
a division of Random House, Inc.
New York

DELACORTE PRESS and colophon are registered trademarks of
Random House, Inc.

www.randomhouse.com/teens

Educators and librarians, for a variety of teaching tools, visit us at
www.randomhouse.com/teachers

Library of Congress Cataloging-in-Publication Data

Wood, Maryrose.
Sex Kittens and Horn Dawgs fall in love / Maryrose Wood. −1st ed.
  p. cm.
  Summary: A group of girls calling themselves the Sex Kittens and their male
counterparts, the Horn Dawgs, face love, karate, and science experiments in an
unstructured private school setting in New York City.
  ISBN 0-385-73276-7 (hardcover) − ISBN 0-385-90296-4 (lib. bdg.)
  [1. High schools−Fiction. 2. Schools−Fiction. 3. Interpersonal relations−
Fiction. 4. Love−Fiction. 5. New York (N.Y.)−Fiction.] I. Title.
  PZ7.W8524Sex 2006
  [Fic]−dc22   2005013659

The text of this book is set in 12-point Baskerville BE Regular.

Book design by Angela Carlino

Printed in the United States of America

10 9 8 7 6 5 4 3 2 1

First Edition

BVG

For Beatrix and Harry,
who taught me the Secret of Love

And for Miguel,
who is a cupcake

ACKNOWLEDGMENTS

Thanks to Elizabeth Kaplan, to Marissa Walsh, and to my early, supportive and very helpful readers: Beatrix Wood Parola, Kate Herzlin, Timothy Mathis, David Johnston, and Andrew Gerle. Thanks to Jacob Gilford for the sitar lesson, and to Rita Wood for the unfailing encouragement. My very special thanks to Emily Jenkins, without whom there would be no Kittens.

1

My Dubious Mental State Gets an Ass-Whupping from the Great Beyond

Kitten meets Dawg. Soon,
A warm yellow rain anoints
The hydrant of love.

"You promised me some animal poems, yes?"

Mr. Frasconi is looking at me with one silvery eyebrow lifted a half-inch higher than the other. You would think I'd know better than to try and pull a fast one on a world-famous poet, but apparently, I don't.

"Um," I say, oozing lameness. "That is an animal poem. Kitten. Dawg. Get it?"

"It's a *love* poem, Fe-li-ci-a." He always gives my

name four syllables. When you're writing a lot of haiku, like I have been lately, you automatically count the syllables in everything. Rice Krispies, three. Matthew Dwyer, four. Mrs. Felicia Dwyer, seven. Not that I'd really take his name once we're married, my mom would go all Gloria Steinem on me.

Mr. Frasconi sees my mind wandering and repeats, for emphasis (insert Meaningful Echo Effect here): "A looooooooove pooooooooeeeemm." Poem, two syllables. Some people think it's one. Not me.

Me, Fe-li-ci-a! Po-et-ess, Total Mess, Felicia the lovelorn. Whose name means happiness, HA!

"This Kitten in your poem, she is you? And the 'Dawg'—interesting spelling—still the same boy? The one with the rabbits?" Mr. Frasconi can never remember Matthew's name, which is odd, since he's been reading my unrequitedly-in-love-with-Matthew poetry since late September and now it's February, and that is like ten zillion poems by now. But I guess I don't call Matthew Matthew in the poems. Usually it's just "him," or "you," or "O, perfect one!" or "unattainable boy of mystery."

"And the 'warm yellow rain'—hmmmm." Yes, thanks to me, Mr. Archibald Frasconi, mega-award-winning poet and currently a Master Mentor at the Manhattan Free Children's School, is being forced to contemplate the symbolic use of pee-pee in a love poem.

Poor Mr. Frasconi. Maybe I should explain the whole Sex Kitten and Horn Dawg thing to him. But a poem has to stand on its own, as Mister Master Mentor himself has often told me, and after some initial resistance I've come to agree with him. You can't follow your poems around explaining them to people, it's just impractical. So, as they say in the cartoons, I shaddup.

Mr. Frasconi leans back in his chair. "No more love poems for a while, okay, Fe-li-ci-a? Look around. Observe. There's so much to see."

There are private schools in this great city where all the students are bored fashionistas and all the teachers are boring fascists.

The Manhattan Free Children's School is NOT one of these schools.

What the MFCS is, instead, is a small private school housed in a crumbly-pretty, pretty crumbly old brownstone near Gramercy Park. And we never call it the MFCS—at least, my friends and I don't. We call it the Pound. Why? Because we are the Kittens, the boys are the Dawgs, so we go to the Pound, get it? And, frankly, it's just too hysterical-making to think of ourselves as the Free Children. I know I go there because my mom is stuck in groovy mode (can somebody please give peace a frikkin chance already, so the poor woman can MOVE ON?), but being the Free Children is too granola for words. We'd much rather be the Sex Kittens, thank you!

Kitten Directive Number Infinity: Kittens Are 4-evah!

Speaking of which:

"It's a perfectly NICE poem. It's just a little—you know! Gross!" Jess says, helpfully.

"Ewww," adds Kat, cutting to the chase.

We are sitting in our favorite booth at the Moonbeam

Diner, Official Restaurant of the Sex Kittens of New York City.

Kitten Directive Number Twenty-three: Any Kitten can convene an Emergency After-School Kittensnack at the Moonbeam to discuss matters of personal urgency. Her littermates will listen, advise, and pounce if necessary, to perform the Kitten Heimlich Maneuver and help said Kitten cough up those painful furballs of self-doubt.

But right now, my fellow Founding Members, Miss Jessica Kornbluth of the Upper West Side and Miss Katarina Arlovsky, born in Moscow but now residing in Washington Heights, are not pouncing or Heimliching. Instead, they are looking at me with looks of extreme dubiosity. As in, Felicia, we have read your little haik-ewww and you need to WAKE UP.

"Really?" I say, feeling tragically misunderstood. "You don't think it's about animals?" Stubborn, I know, not my best quality. But Mr. Frasconi kind of bummed me out by kiboshing the Matthew poems, and if your two tightest Kittenpals can't see your side of things, who can?

Jess has an unusually animated face and way of talking, and her eyebrows achieve serious altitude when she's expressing any strong emotion (sort of like Mr. Frasconi's, come to think of it). Right now they look like they're about to fire their booster rockets and bust a move out of the atmosphere. "Fee," she says, in her listen-to-me tone of voice. "I'm no poet, but I think Mr. Frasconi's point MIGHT be that you are spending way, way, WAY too much energy on this THING, you know, this nonexistent THING with Matthew, and maybe, just MAYBE you should take a BREAK!"

4

"You're obsessed," says Kat darkly. She's chewing on her hair, which she quit doing a year ago because it gave her split ends. "Obsession is dangerous. People go insane."

"The syllables are perfect, though!" Jess adds. "Five-seven-five, that's awesome!"

I am about to feign huffiness and get all don't-count-syllables-to-me, but for one thing the Moonie arrives with our food (all the waitstaff here at the Moonbeam Diner wear black T-shirts with big yellow cheesy moons on them), and for another thing—

Could they be RIGHT?

Am I not only obsessed with Matthew, but skipping merrily down the garden path to kookooland?

There is only one way to find out.

Felicia's Private Kitten Directive Number Eleventy-seven (insert New Age Music Suggestive of Imminent Communication with Unseen Forces here): When in doubt, consult the Oracle!

What is this Oracle, you ask? To answer that we must time-travel back to late September, when the whole Sex Kitten thing started. September was when, and as for where: it happened at my mom's bookstore, the Unbound Page. The store is right in the heart of New York City's Bohemian Central, the East Villahge, near Tompkins Square Park and only two blocks from the humble digs Momski and I call home. (Dad currently re-sides in New Jersey with "Laura," excuse me, what kind of a soapstar name is THAT?)

My mom opened the Unbound Page right before I was born, and in fourteen years it's evolved into a neighborhood treasure trove of esoterica and interdimensional grooviness. It has sections like Relaxology: Chilling Your Soul-Self Out, and Runes and Tunes: The Music of Ancient Wisdom. My mom believes that most people are just very very tense, and that's why there's war and unhappiness and bad skin.

O, historic Kitten-making day! It was only three weeks after the start of the fall semester, and out of all the frosh students at the Pound, Jess and Kat and I were least freaked out by our new school's delightful lack of schoolness. The rest seemed temporarily short-circuited by the absence of tests, grades, classes, and homework, and walked around muttering: "Why do the teachers ignore us unless we collar them with a question, and are you sure we can just leave during the day without telling anyone?" But though we had just met, we three shared the d'lishus suspicion that just being ourselves, fearless and fourteen, with all of New York City at our feet, was bound to be education enough for anyone.

Initial shell shock aside, the Pound does tend to attract an unusual type of student, and even among us clueless newbies nearly everybody already had a "thing." As in, my thing is poetry, and Matthew's thing is science and the genius rabbits, and Kat's thing is music, and Jess's thing is saving the world. The bookstore is my mom's thing, and since Jess and Kat and I were hitting it off, I figured they'd appreciate it. And so, we went.

"What's this?" Kat asked, picking up a boxed deck of tarot cards. My mom kinda frowns on the whole fortune-telling aspect of esoterica, but it sells.

"The Deck of Pets," read Jess off the box. "A Tarot for Animals and Their Human Slaves. A Portion of Our Profits Goes to the ASPCA. That is SO cool!"

"The Beanie Deck," read Kat, picking up another box. "Look! It's all Beanie Babies!" Kat tends to be quite serious, but this made her giggle. I have to admit, it was pretty hilarious imagining a whole tarot of Beanie Babies juggling coins and throwing wands and stuff.

And while we were laughing about the Beanies and I personally was feeling glad that my new friends were displaying the appropriate mix of coolness and whimsy–

–the Oracle REVEALED itself!

All the other decks were boxed and shrink-wrapped; otherwise, customers would riffle through them till the cards were too worn around the edges to sell (shelf wear, my mom calls this; I used to think it was some strange bookstore fashion requirement, like cruise wear). But this deck was just sitting out, unwrapped and brand-spanking-new. It didn't occur to me till later that it was freaky that I'd never seen it before, freakier still because I'm in the bookstore practically every day.

"Look," I said, turning it over. "The Tarot of Kittens."

"Awwwwwwwwww!" Our laughter melted into the universal isn't-that-cute noise all at once, like we planned it. I mean, okay, everybody loves kittens. But THESE kittens were just so esoterically irresistible. Cute to the point of spooky, if I may coin such a phrase.

We went through the deck card by card, each picture more weirdly heart-tugging than the next. The Kitten of Cups. The Queen of Kittens. The Death Kitten (that was a fluffy white one staring hungrily into a goldfish bowl).

And then, not even thinking, I said, "Okay, cards! What does the future hold for US?" I flipped over the next card, and there it was.

The Sex Kittens! Three adorable baby kitties nestled in a strappy, sexy high-heel shoe. The text on the bottom of the card said something about the life force and connection and rebirth, but we were too busy screaming with laughter. My mom even came over to see what was up, but all we could do was point and scream louder. She brought us glasses of lemonade and didn't ask questions, my mom's kinda cool that way.

So that's how we became, and remain, the Sex Kittens. We are not sluts, nor do we dress like jailbait-porno-pop-stars, navels to the wind. But during the weeks that followed (and naturally, after an experience like that we KNEW we were indisputably the best of friends 4-evah!), Kat and Jess and I agreed that we are each juicy and beautiful in a unique, one-of-a-kind kind of way, so the Oracle was right and Sex Kittens are obviously what we must be, matters of wardrobe and relative boob size notwithstanding.

Kitten Directive Number Thirty-nine: Kittens ROCK!

Now, just in case you're starting to think we're silly, superstitious girls with too much homework-free time on our hands to spend making up kittycat nicknames, don't. I won't speak of myself, but apart from Matthew (sigh!) Dwyer, I would say Jessica Kornbluth is the most purely rational person I know, and Katarina Arlovksy is one of the hardest-working (not to mention talented), and neither one of them is the least bit silly except in a fun-loving way. But it's not every day you jump up and get a high five from the Great Beyond, and that's what this was. (Okay, SkeptiKitten Jess retained the right to interpret it as a metaphor, but whateva-4!)

Once we were the Sex Kittens, it was a very short leap to realize that our mysterious cotravelers, occasional pals, and frequent *objets* of Kittenish affection—that is to say, *les garçons*—could be none other than the Horn Dawgs (*excusez-moi* for that quickie French vocabulary review, but I have to squeeze my education in somehow). So our school became the Pound, we're-Kittens-and-Dawgs-so-we-live-in-a-Pound, get-it-get-it, and, I mean, this all makes perfect sense, right?

So, *pardonnez-moi, Monsieur Frasconi,* but I STILL don't understand why it's not an animal poem!

Obsession is dangerous. People go insane.
Shaddup, brain. I'm looking for the Oracle.
After today's Moonbeam meeting, my feelings of being tragically misunderstood about the haik-ewww now overshadowed by the fresh worry that I might be mentally ill, I hightail it to the M15 bus and whiz downtown to the bookstore. Off the bus, past the vintage dress shop, the body piercing/tattoo parlor, and the take-out falafel place I go. Through the door of the Unbound Page (insert a soothing *ding-dong* of wind chimes here), a quick wave at Motherdear, who's at the cash register with a customer, and straight to the Tarot of Kittens.

Am I sickly and weirdly obsessed with Matthew and in need of a serious reality check and maybe some meds? Or are Matthew and I karmically preordained to be in looooooooooove and it's just that I realized it first and he's taking his slow, sweet time to come around to the cosmic inevitable? These are the questions I plan to ask the Oracle.

Once I find it, that is.

"What are you looking for, honey?"

I always hide the Oracle behind something else, like a book of Chinese astrology or a copy of *Find Your Inner Goddess Archetype Within That's Inside You*. (At one point I had considered buying the Oracle, or just asking my mom to give it to me, but I decided that would diminish its mojo. No One Can Own the Portal to the Great Beyond!)

"Felicia, what are you doing?"

But it's not here.

"FELICIA!" The customer has gone, I hear the mellow Tibetan wind chimes ring as the door shuts. Mom is staring at me like I've been ignoring her or something.

"I can't find the Kitten deck," I say.

"The Tarot of Kittens?" she asks. "Cute deck. I just sold it. Why didn't you tell me you wanted it?"

Because that would diminish its mojo, Mom-o! But I can't say that. I'm speechless. The Oracle is gone, just when I needed it!

(I am actually the only one of the Sex Kittens who's maintained an attachment to the Kitten deck. When Jess has pressing life questions she asks herself, "What would Gandhi do?" and Kat just practices her violin till her fingers bleed and then she feels better. But I have consulted, the Oracle regularly. Does Matthew love me yet? How about today? Will he ever love me? Et sweatera.)

(Et sweatera, by the way, is Kat's expression for

when you're giving a recital and you're nervous and can't stop sweating and so you put on a sweater over your sleeveless gown to hide the sweat and that just makes it worse, et sweatera.)

Mom sees my panic attack and sighs. "There are thirty other decks here, Felicia, what's the big deal?"

Can you understand why I might not have shared with Motherdear that my friends and I call ourselves the Sex Kittens? Mom is cool, but no mom is THAT cool.

Before I can say anything, she puts her hands over my eyes. "Here," she says. "Calm down for a minute. Say to yourself, 'The Kitten deck already gave me its gift. Now I'm ready for fresh wisdom.' "

"Kittengiftreadyfreshwisdom," I mumble.

"Choose a new deck. No peeking," she says, clamping her hands tighter over my eyes.

I reach my hands out, run my fingertips over the shrink-wrapped boxes. I stop, exhale. "This one," I say. The Oracle isn't gone, I tell myself. It's just changed portals. My questions will be answered and everything will be fine and Matthew will *lovemelovemeloveme*. . . .

"The Tarot of Hollywood Stars!" Mom says, handing me the box. There's a picture of Clint Eastwood on the cover. Obviously, the Death card.

"Ewwww," I say.

"Don't judge." Mom smooches me on the head. "Be open. You'll learn something." Mom considers "being open" one of the cardinal virtues. This was a big problem in her relationship with Dad. Dad is not "open" enough for her.

Near the front of the store, a customer is struggling to

get one of the big laminated acupuncture charts down off a high shelf. "I gotta go," says Mom, tearing the shrink-wrap off the deck and handing it to me. "Have fun."

The Tarot of Hollywood Stars? Puh-leeze. I'm this-close to putting the deck back on the shelf and going home and writing some really stalkerish love poems, just for spite. But—what's the harm in choosing a card or two?

I close my eyes and shuffle. I think of Matthew, and I ask: sick obsession, or lovahDawg of destiny? I turn over a card.

Johnny Depp. Frikkin cute, that Johnny Depp. I read:

THE OBJECT OF YOUR DESIRE SEEMS PERFECT AND UNATTAINABLE. NEITHER IS TRUE. SEEK THE SUBSTANCE BENEATH A CAREFULLY CONSTRUCTED IMAGE.

Huh. A simple yes or no would have been good. Seek the substance. Do they mean chocolate? Get serious, Felicia, this is MATTHEW we're talking about!

I think of Matthew: his cool gray eyes, the silky hair that falls in his face a hundred times a day, the way he murmurs little secret things to the rabbits he keeps at school.

I concentrate, close my eyes, choose another card.

The Olsen twins. Feh. This deck is an embarrassment to all things esoteric. But I read:

IN ORDER TO MAKE TWO INTO ONE, ABANDON YOUR FIXED IDEAS. INSTEAD, SEE THE WORLD THROUGH THE EYES OF YOUR PARTNER. A FRESH APPROACH IS NEEDED.

Okay, a fresh approach, but what-what-WHAT? A clue, *s'il vous plaît*! One more card and that's it; this is making me even more mental and that was not my goal.

I think of Matthew: it's like there is some mysterious THING that I am so PATHETICALLY LACKING that, if I could only figure out what it is and *get* some, would change everything and then Matthew would love me like I love him, happy ending and fade out in a little heart shape.

Is there such a thing? And if so, what is it?

I choose a third card.

It's Meg Ryan.

Meg Ryan. I thought we said Hollywood STARS. This must be an old deck. I look for the text.

There is no text.

But all the cards have text.

ALL THE CARDS EXCEPT MEG RYAN.

"Get off the phone, honey, the movie's gonna start!"

"So what does that mean?–just PAUSE it, Mom!–I mean, no text at all? That's weird, right?"

Jess is on the other end of the phone, listening patiently to my hysteria. She was not nearly as disturbed as I was about the Kitten deck being sold. In fact, she seemed to find it wonderfully mysterious.

"I don't know, Fee." Jess is the only person who calls me Fee. It saves her time, which is important to her. "I guess it means you have to figure it out yourself."

"That is some lazy-butted Oracle, then!"

"Felicia!" Mom's patience has run out.

"Okay, okay, gotta go. See ya tomorrow."

"Okay. And, hey, Fee–happy Valentine's Day!"

I hang up the phone. Ohmigod.
Ohmiblessedinnergoddessarchetypewithinthat'sin-
sideme.

Why does today have to be Valentine's Day?

Not just because today is the day the true Oracle
abandoned me and sent a bunch of cheesy Hollywood
has-beens in its place, except for Johnny Depp, who is a
cupcake.

And not just because I've been CRAZY-IN-LOVE-
WITH-MATTHEW-DWYER for six months and there
is nothing to show for it except my own increasingly dubious mental state, plus ten zillion poems that are—sorry,
Mr. Frasconi—not about animals.

No, my question is more general. Why does it have
to be Valentine's Day, EVER?

Isn't February bad enough? It's dark and cold and
slushy and yucky, even in my beloved Big Frozen
Apple, and then comes this pointless annual exercise in
cruelty and mockery, which I do my best to block out.
(Recall how, during my tête-à-tête-à-tête with the Kittens
today, I never mentioned the little red foil hearts strung
around the Moonbeam? Or the single red roses in bud
vases, pathetically wilting on each table? Or how our
Moonie had red glitter stuck to her cheek in a foolish little heart shape? That's because I didn't see any of it,
that's how powerful my blocking mechanism is. Yes, impressive, I know.)

Valentine's Day, date-night U.S.A. for the boyfriended,
how nice for them, on a Thursday night the calendar
says I should be having dinner with my dad. But this
week he and "Laura" are off snorkeling in Bermuda,
how extremely nice for them, while Mom and I sit here

in our no-boys-allowed East Village chick pad with our spoils from Blockbuster: *Terminator 2,* in which a single mom with no body fat whups everybody's ass, hmmm, I wonder why Motherdear never tires of it?

Did I mention cruelty and mockery? As I hang up with Jess and plop my butt on the phuton couch (Jess once read an old novel where sofa was spelled "sopha" throughout, so now we spell futon "phuton"), I can see that, appallingly, the *Terminator* tape has started with a trailer for some mushy loooooooove movie. Like that's really what I need to be seeing right now.

"*Sleepless in Seattle*! This must be an old tape," Mom says, crunching on some popcorn. "All the DVDs were out, can you believe it?" Sure I can. It means we're not the only losers—sorry, people—in New York City who are home watching movies tonight.

Wait. Waitwaitwait. Sleepless in SEATTLE?

Isn't that a MEG RYAN movie?

It is—there she is, all tiny and love-struck on the TV screen, all young and goofy and pretty, her hair all freakishly fluffy in that Meg Ryan way!

This Kitten ZAPS to attention. My arms go goose bumpy. The Oracle is about to speak!

I concentrate as hard as I can on my question: what is the thing that would make Matthew *lovemelovemeloveme* if I weren't so pathetically lacking whatever this thing is? And does such a thing even exist, and what is it, and HOW DO I GET IT? Okay, three questions, but whatever! Speak, Oracle! I'm listening!

"Meg Ryan has IT." Mom's mouth is full of popcorn, but I could swear that's what she said.

"Meg Ryan has what?" I ask, trying so very hard

to sound casual. Mom chews. I want to yank the bowl of popcorn away. Oracles should not talk with their mouths full.

Mom picks a little kernel off her front tooth. Gross, Mom.

"You know. IT," she says. "The X-factor of love. Ohhhhh, yes. Meg Ryan is the walking embodiment." My mom says things like "walking embodiment" the way other people say "nice day, isn't it?" I actually admire that about her.

"Think of any Meg Ryan movie," she goes on, waxing profound. "As soon as she comes on-screen, it's like a flock of demented Disney lovebirds start fluttering around her. The lighting gets woozy, the music swells. Is there ANY chance this woman is NOT going to get the guy she wants? I mean, come on!"

Mom takes another sip of Shiraz. I say this not to suggest that she is a drinker of any repute, because she is so totally not. But she's on a bit of a roll about this Meg Ryan thing, and the half-glass of wine she's consumed in preparation for our Valentine's extravaganza is no doubt making some small contribution. That and the fact that she's serving as a mouthpiece for the Great Beyond.

I, meanwhile, am truly impressed at the way the Oracle has taken possession of my mother AND my TV. The answer to my question is coming through loud as a rock drummer and clear as Sprite (insert Booming Oracular Voice here): "Yes, Felicia, there is an IT! A love catnip! An X-factor of loooooove!"

I began wondering what Matthew (O be mine!) Dwyer is doing right this very Valentine's minute. Oh, the love catnip I would waggle under his precious nose, if only I had some—

Mom looks at me, oozing maternitude. "But that's just in the movies, honey," she coos, leaning in—is this her talking, or the Greater Forces of All-Knowingness? "Real life," she intones, "is more complicated."

My goose bumps fade. I'm 99 percent sure that was Mom talking; I can tell by the way she sinks back on the phuton with that pleased, I've-Bonded-with-My-Teenage-Daughter expression on her face. The Oracle has shaddup and the Feature Presentation is about to begin. *Mominator 2.*

Mom says every line before the characters do, and chuckles to herself afterward. This is what passes for entertainment around here. I'm only pretending to watch the movie, because all my inward energies are scrunched in a ball, playing and replaying the mysterious Meg Ryan message:

IT...

Love catnip...

The X-factor of loooooove...

Before you can say Ahhhhhnold, Humanity has been saved from the Machines once more, and Maman is rinsing out her wineglass and yawning and giving me the old tapping-her-watch, meaningful Mom-eye. As if she had not recently served as a popcorn-chewing bullhorn for the Great Beyond!

I have some serious thinking to do, so I smooch the old girl good night and retire for the evening. This involves walking exactly eight steps, through the Living/Dining/Home Office/Multipurpose Space that is the main part of our apartment, through the short hallway, and into the little bathroom with the pull-chain light, and then into My Own Room.

(Mom sleeps on a Murphy bed in the L/D/HO/Multipurpose Et sweatera, and she is a total sweetie pie to let me have the bedroom. "A girl your age needs privacy, so you can develop your *autonomy*," she has said on more than one occasion. Autonomy has nothing to do with getting a car, but we city folk prefer the trains and buses anyway. Why travel alone?)

I sleep on a twin-size phuton with midnight blue sheets and a crimson velvet bedspread that I think was a stage curtain once. I dig around for my stretched-out black yoga pants and an ancient Hello Kitty T-shirt, grab my notebook and favorite pen, and climb into bed.

Now to work. The X-factor of love DEFINITELY exists, the Oracle made that as plain as a pair of chinos from Land's End. But what is it? And how do I get some?

I start to make notes. Johnny Depp. The Olsen twins. Meg Ryan.

See the world through the eyes of your partner. . . . A fresh approach is needed. . . .

But how can I see the world through Matthew's eyes? All he cares about is science!

Felicia's Private Kitten Directive Number Tensy-thirteen: When in doubt, sleep on it. Answers often come in dreams.

Here's the poem I wrote that night, before I fell asleep. It does not even pretend to be an animal poem.

Love makes people nervous wrecks.
You often see them cryin'.
Their love connection disconnects,
And not for lack of tryin'.
It's like there is some evil hex
That turns true love to lyin'.
If only we could all ooze X,
Just like Meg Ryan.

2

Against All Advice, I Tell Matthew
That I Have Something to Tell Him

Let us pause for a moment and be thankful for dreams, visions, and the restorative powers of sleep.

Thank you.

And for the fact that there are no coincidences.

Thank YOU!

For Mere Coincidence could NEVER explain how, this morning, as I yawned and stretched and rummaged through my stage-curtain bedspread for my notebook, the sunlight that comes through the narrow window above my bed only for an hour a day and only during the winter months, when the sun lines up just so with the crack between the two tenements behind our building (our own East Village Stonehenge, Mom likes to joke)—what else but FATE could possibly explain how those scarce and carefully timed photons (as opposed to phutons!) zoomed through the glass and cut a beam of bright, dancing dust particles in the air before landing precisely on the life-changing words I scribbled last night, like a sunshine yellow Highlighter of Destiny:

But how can I see the world through Matthew's eyes? All he cares about is science!

And twin thank-yous to you and you, Ashley and Mary-Kate Olsen! *Merci, merci* for the following invaluable tip!

In order to make two into one . . . see the world through the eyes of your partner. . . .

Matthew and I will be sure to invite both of you to the wedding.

To review: I am, first and foremost, a poet.

But in the case of Me and Matthew, it will not be a sonnet or a limerick or a haiku, not Shakespeare or Emily Dickinson or even Anonymous who will provide the Secret Decoder Ring of Loooooooooove.

It will be SCIENCE.

WHAT IS X?

X (also known as IT, but X sounds more Scientific and that is the KEY!) is the thing that makes Love Work Out. X is what makes soulmates recognize each other across crowded rooms and turns just-friends into the love-of-my-life, never had a fight and pass me another slice of that 50th anniversary cake, puh-leeze!

Most importantly, X is what gives a Sex Kitten guaranteed, ongoing proximity to a Horn Dawg. The math on this is très simple:

$$Kitten + Dawg + X$$
$$= \text{strolling in the park As One,}$$
$$\text{hand snuggling in hand}$$
$$= \text{lunching together in the cafeteria,}$$
$$\text{tray nuzzling against tray}$$
$$= \text{being envied by the envious throngs}$$
$$\text{who think of you as a Permanently}$$
$$\text{Melded Couple—FeliciaMatthew, or}$$
$$\text{MatthewFelicia, for example.}$$

X is a Total Mystery, an Unnamed Source, a Top Secret Classified Document with all the juicy parts crossed out. X has blocked its Caller ID and hangs up before leaving a message.

BUT by using the cold, rational, completely objective tools of SCIENTIFIC research, I am going to unmask the meaning of X and discover the Secret of Love.

And Matthew Dwyer, Boy Scientist and GeniusDawg of Data, is going to help me.

P.S. He does not know this. Yet.
I'm going to tell him today.

"You're going to do WHAT?"

Jess is looking at me with those alarmingly raised eyebrows. Her mouth is open, too, in a perfectly round shape. She looks like a cartoon of a surprised person.

Kat has remembered that she no longer chews her hair. She is now sucking on the tassel of her scarf. "You are too much, Felicia," she says. "Too. Much." This is tough talk from Kat, who thinks more but says less than most people.

I knew Jess and Kat would need some time to rally round the Scientific Search for X. Early this morning, after my visit from the Yellow Highlighter of Destiny and before I got in the shower, I dashed off the first draft of my X-cellent Manifesto (see above) and e-mailed the Kittens a sneak preview. With fingers Xed, you might say, since I know my worried pals are reaching the limits of their patience when it comes to my obsess—whoops, my feelings about Matthew.

"I guess you got my e-mail," I say in my what's-the-big-deal voice. Now truly fearing for my sanity, Jess and Kat have intercepted me at Third Avenue where the M15 bus lets me off. We're rounding the corner of East Nineteenth and Irving Place, right at the point where the Pound comes into view.

It's a bright, sparkly winter morning, and the sun is melting what's left of the snow into dirt-flavored Slurpee. The Pound has these funny curved windows up the front of its five brownstone stories. If the light is in the right place and you squint, it looks like the building is smiling at you, like the man in the moon smiles at you wherever you go. The building looks like that now. I take that as a good sign.

But Jess is not smiling. Those expressive eyebrows have furrowed low over her darkest brown, almost black eyes. Jess sometimes looks like Little Orphan Annie, with her frizzed reddish-brown hair and dot eyes. I mean that in a good way. She'd never describe herself as cute, but she is, even when she's stomping through slush and ranting, like so:

"Fee, LISTEN. I think you are making a BIG mistake. Number one, you are obsessed."

"People go insane," adds Kat.

"Number two, once you TELL him, you can never UN-tell him! You will have to LIVE with the consequences of this CONFESSION until we are SENIORS!" I think she means senior year, but Jess is always so EMPHATIC in her OPINIONS that maybe she means senior citizens. (Jess is planning to go to law school someday so she can make the world a better place. I think it's a FINE plan.)

Kat is staring at her boots as if they're interesting. She glances up at me—up from the boots, I mean, but actually down, since she's a good five inches taller than me.

"I just don't know, Felicia," she says, barely audible.

Which is the last straw. Enough! "Look," I say. "The Search for X is NOT what you think!"

What I want to say is this:

Hear me, O Kittens! Is it right that I should spend these precious days of my fourteenth year moping, pining, wondering, and waiting for a smoke signal of looooove from Matthew Dwyer, Dawg-o'-my-dreams?

Is it fair that I should be exerting so much of my Kittenpowers purring hopefully in his direction, with only the most feeble of tail wags in return?

No. It is not. So I have to DO something. Even the Oracle thinks so. Anything would be better than this LIFE OF TORMENT.

But that sounds so deeply loseresque, so what I actually say is: "Yes! I'm going to tell Matthew how I feel about him. But it's not the pathetic stalker move it sounds like!"

We've arrived at the Pound. The Free Children are milling about, trying to make wet gray snowballs out of the mush. Kat is looking at her feet again. Miss Jessica Kornbluth for the Prosecution has crossed her arms. That's never a good sign.

"And even if it is, it's for the sake of science!" I blather on. "Matthew's a scientist. This is something that will add to the body of human knowledge. I'm sure he'll totally understand." And not think I'm a geeky, X-deficient loser, I neglect to add—out loud, anyway.

Neither Jess nor Kat is looking at me at all now. They're both focusing on something a little above and behind my right shoulder.

"And NOT think I'm a geeky, X-deficient LOSER!" I decide to say, borrowing some of Jess's emphaticness for emphasis.

"Hey." It's a Dawgvoice. "Hi, Jessica. Hi, Katarina."

I'm wondering exactly what shade of red my face is, but it's a moot point, since you can't RIP your face off your head and hide it in your backpack, even if you desperately want to for some humiliating reason.

"Hi, Felicia," says the Dawgvoice.

Exhale a *whew* of relief! It's only Randall. Randall is perfectly nice but dull, the sort of person you would not even notice except he's best friends and Dawgbuddies with Matthew Dwyer. On his own merits, Randall's not the sort of Dawg your face should get red about saying something stupid in front of.

(Mr. Frasconi would prefer I say Randall's not the

sort of Dawg in front of whom your face should get red. But I like it better my way.)

Nope, Randall's definitely not the sort of Dawg whose unexpected arrival would make your cheeks turn strawberry ice cream color, but not cool like ice cream, more hot like tomato soup, no matter how much of a fool you might have just been acting like (sorry, Mr. F!).

Unless, of course, shoot-me-now Matthew Dwyer was standing RIGHT BEHIND HIM.

Yes, there's my cutieDawg standing there, skinny and slouched like a greyhound in the cold morning sun. Hair the color of winter grass in Central Park, and soft as a rabbit's ear. At least, I imagine it is. I've never actually touched Matthew's hair.

Jess and Kat are looking at me with that mixture of horror and fascination usually reserved for watching reality television. Now that she's eaten a teacup full of slugs, what will that madcap Felicia do next? I do not disappoint.

"Hey, Matthew."

"Hey," he says.

"Listen," I say, smiling the smile of a used-car salesman with a lemon to unload, the useless, nothing-left-to-lose smile of a death row inmate slurping down one final milk shake. "I have a really cool idea for a, um, science thing. Can I talk to you about it?"

At the words "science thing," Matthew perks up like a puppy that just spotted his lost chew toy under the phuton.

"What is it?" he says in his yummy, quiet voice.

"Are you gonna be in the lab later? It's kind of complicated. I'll come by and we can—"

I pause for effect, and also to enjoy the sight of Jess sputtering and Kat, who generally avoids eye contact, just outright staring at me. "You know. *Talk* about it."

Matthew nods. "Sure. I have to clean all the rabbit cages today, so I'll be there, like, all afternoon."

Okay cool, cool, later, see ya later. Phase one is complete! How easy is this? X, prepare to surrender your mystery. The Secret of Love is an onion that just lost one layer of skin.

This afternoon, I will go to the lab, and there, as we breathe in the fragrant bunny-turd aroma of the rabbit hutches, I will tell Matthew all the things that I have, um, decided to tell him.

Felicia's Private Kitten Directive Number Gazillion: When your Kittenpals tell you you're insane, YOU ARE.

I AM INSANE.

Uh, Jess? Kat?

WHY DIDN'T YOU STOP ME???????

3

Tick, Tock. Tick, Tock. The Longest Morning of One Kitten's Life

During a typical day at the Pound, all us Free Children are supposed to pass the time by digging deeply into our passions, creating our own learning plans, being self-directed and self-motivated and self-self-self. This approach to education offers many advantages, such as the opportunity to spend your day writing love poetry (like me) or breeding genius rabbits (like Matthew). But it is a huge problem when you are in a state of, yes, OBSESSIVE anxiety about a chain of potentially humiliating events you have just set in motion and inside your self is the last place you want to be.

Luckily, there's no rule that says I can't spend the

morning tagging along as my fellow Poundmates engage in the self-directed pursuit of their self-induced passions. And no one is more self-directed and passionate than—

"Why is it so hard to just HELP people? I mean, I'm trying to do something NICE! And she looked at me like I was there to steal her LUNCH or something!" So says Jessica Kornbluth, founder of and (so far) sole participant in the brand-new MFCS Peer Tutoring Outreach Program. We're in the second-floor kitchen of the Pound. (The building used to be some rich person's house, and it still feels more like an eccentric old mansion than a school—there are kitchens and sitting rooms and a creaky, tiny elevator with a black iron gate that's hard to close, so we prefer the narrow, twisty back stairways that sneak you from floor to floor.)

Jessica "Helping People Is My Thing" Kornbluth is helping herself to a nice foamy cup of coffee with steamed milk. Two shakes of cinnamon, one shake of cocoa. Her mug sports a faded picture of Captain Kirk and Mr. Spock and Dr. McCoy standing in the transporter chamber. They're supposed to appear and disappear based on the temperature of the mug, but that was a million rides through the dishwasher ago, and now they're just permanently semi-materialized, which I imagine would tickle.

But those are my thoughts. I doubt Jess is concerned about Captain Kirk's discomfort; she has Serious Real-Life Issues on her mind, always. She tucks her very organized, businesslike black binder under her arm, with all its pert little color-coded tabs sticking out, and heads for the Red Room.

There are a few sitting-room areas on each of the Pound's five mazelike floors, but our favorite is the Red

Room, so called because of the floor-length cherry red drapes hanging at the south window. I'm feeling calmer already, curled up on the Red Room's squishy old sopha, staring into the huge marble fireplace and soaking up that brisk, everything's-under-control vibe Jess gives off. Maybe I should get a binder, too. Section One: Things Matthew Has Said to Me and What They Might Mean. Section Two: Stupid Things I Have Said to Others That Matthew Might Have Overheard. Section Three: Favorite Foods. Section Four—

Jess flips her binder open with a loud snap. "That's her," she says. "My first student. I mean, peer learning partner."

I look at the neatly typewritten form and read:

NAME: *Doris Jean ("D.J.") Amberson*
SCHOOL: *East Harlem Vocational High School, NYC*
GRADE: *9*
WHY DO YOU WANT A PEER LEARNING PARTNER?
My mama and daddy and especially Grandma Doris say I am not learning bo-diddley at this run-down overcrowded excuse of a school.
SPECIAL INTERESTS:

Here there was something written but scribbled over. Underneath the scribble, in a different handwriting, it said:

Stuck-up Priss Doris Jean has not one interest that's special, thank you now go away! XOXOXOX S&D

"Fascinating, isn't it? I wonder who S and D are!" Jess says. She closes her binder and beams, looking genuinely pleased. "This is going to be a CHALLENGE!"

Jess drains the last of her drink, creating a tiny milk-foam mustache on her lip. "I'd better go. I'm supposed to meet her during her lunch period and her school is way uptown."

"Bonne chance!" I say, handing her a napkin. We're such good pals she doesn't even blink, she just wipes the foam off her mouth and looks at me.

"Good luck to you, too, Fee." I'm glad Jess has stopped yelling at me about this Matthew thing. I guess she realizes I'm beyond help.

Kitten Directive Number Eighty-six: Stand By Your Littermates, No Matter What!

Jess smiles. "No matter what happens," she says, like she heard what I was thinking, "he is one lucky Dawg to have YOU interested in HIM. Remember that!"

And Kitten Kornbluth trots out to do battle, binder tucked under her arm.

Like a milk mustache,
Faint traces of you persist.
Love leaves evidence.

To be technically correct, a haiku is supposed to make some reference to nature. The cherry blossoms, the melting frost, the baby frogs peeping foolishly in the swamp until the crane gobbles them up–these are supposed to let the reader know what time of year it is. That is the tradition, anyway, and perhaps it is relevant and meaningful in Japan, where the weather turns from winter to spring, summer to fall, providing many opportunities for haiku poets to sprinkle seasonal references on their work, like blueberries on Cheerios.

Here in New York City, there are only two seasons. Coat and no-coat. Some would argue that there are brief jacket seasons in between and that these happy, mild weeks provide the best opportunities for attractively layered outfits. True, but these weeks are fleeting and purely transitional in nature. If you're counting actual seasons, we're talking two and only two.

What does this mean for New York poets working in the haiku form? References to coat and no-coat are certainly possible, but in my experience they lack the symbolic oomph of the blossom, the frog, and the crane. Variations, like sock season versus pedicure season, only make matters worse. Mr. Frasconi, though initially confused by my persistent questions on this subject, did finally come to agree with me. So I don't trouble myself with the seasonal tradition when writing haiku. Counting syllables is enough entertainment for me.

"ONE-two-three-four-five, ONE-two-three-four-five—*bleeping blintzsky Kremlin bleepsky!*" A stream of furious Russian swearwords carries through the door of the practice room.

Often, when I'm looking for a quiet place to write, or think, or frantically OBSESS about some Matthew-related issue, I go down to the basement of the Pound, where there are a dozen small, not-quite-soundproof rooms used by the musically inclined Free Children for practicing. Even if the rooms are all in use, for some reason I find the narrow, fluorescent-lit hallway with its scratchy synthetic carpet an inviting place to camp out. Plus, Kat's almost always down here practicing, and I never tire of hearing her swear in Russian.

That's right, quiet Kat! Cusses like a merchant sailor on the Baltic Sea, like a KGB agent who can't get a signal on his shoe phone, but only when she has her violin in hand. She has quite a repertoire (of Russian profanity, I mean). When I ask her what the words mean, she just looks at me. "It's so obscene," she'll say gravely, "it's *untranslatable*."

Like New York weather, Kat comes in two seasons. No-Violin Kat is shy and says as little as possible, but Violin Kat looks you straight in the eye when she talks, stomps her foot when she's frustrated, yells filth in Russian when she makes a mistake, and practices, practices, practices. Especially when she has a recital coming up, which she does.

I wonder if I could find some magic object, like Kat's violin, that would render me invincible on demand? My problem (like I only have ONE!) is that I think of things that make perfect sense inside my own head (where, like any poet, I spend a lot of time). But when these ideas get LOOSE and are all of a sudden lying there in the cruel light of day, the perfect sense part goes *pfffft!* All gone.

Right now, as the minutes separating Me from Doom tick-tock away, that's how I'm feeling about the Search for X. I mean, WHAT was I thinking? Wouldn't it be easier, and in fact totally preferable, to leave things with Matthew the way they are? Me pining and yearning, him oblivious? It's not an ideal relationship, but it's something, right?

Kat opens the door of the practice room. She's breathless, as if she's just done fifty jumping jacks. She's holding her violin. Watch out.

"Felicia! What are you doing here?" She looks at me with the crazed eyes of someone who just got out of the Bach Violin Concerto No. 2 in E Major alive, but barely. "Why are you hiding here in the basement? I thought you were going upstairs to confess your love to Matthew—"

"I am! Later!" I interrupt. Thinking about it is unbearable. "Now I'm just, you know. Writing poems and stuff. You sound good today," I add lamely.

"I sound TERRIBLE! I'm going to smash my violin into a thousand pieces and set the pieces on fire and never, ever play again!" She wipes her sweaty forehead with her sleeve. "Do you want to come in?"

What I want is to hold that magic violin and suck up all its mojo, make myself stop thinking, and just be fearless and foolhardy in the name of love! But that's asking a lot.

Kat rarely lets me in the room with her while she's practicing, so I know this is a special invitation. I enter the sacred cubicle and close the door behind me.

"Do you want me to turn pages or something?" I ask. She turns her back to the music stand.

"Just sit there," she says. "I think I have it memorized. It's going to sound like *bleeping borscht paprika bleepsky,* but I don't care right now. The goal is not to stop."

The goal is not to stop. Hmmmmm. This sentence activates the philosopher-poet centers of my brain in a pleasant, provocative way. I turn it over in my mind as Kat cues her imaginary accompanist with a look, inhales sharply, and begins to play.

X X X

I spotted Matthew on my very first day at the Pound. I was in the gungest of gung-ho moods that day, quite pleased at having survived the less-than-stimulating early years of my education, which I did by perfecting a kind of dreamy daze. Now I was hoping for something more.

(To summarize: two years of fancy private preschool; then my parents split up and I switched to public school, where I spent another two years drawing ponies and writing verse novels while the other kids were getting hooked on phonics, which drove my mom insane, which led to a year of homeschooling, which was fun because I basically sat around and read my way through the bookstore, but Mom was all guilt ridden because she had to deal with the customers and couldn't do lots of "educational" stuff with me, so back to public school for a final, dreamy-dazed shift before I was old enough for the Pound.)

Was it the way his long limbs struck weird angles when he sat cross-legged on the floor? Or the quiet-but-not-shy voice he used to ask questions during orientation, like "Will I be able to access the lab during holiday breaks?" (The rest of us were very curious as to why he would need to do that, but that was before we knew about the genius rabbit project.)

What was it about Matthew that made him stand out in the crowd, a vivid Fujicolor Dawg in a sea of half-ripe Polaroids? I knew I couldn't take my eyes off him, but why?

I can't answer, of course, because the answer is X. Matthew, obviously, has X. Tons of X. Gives it off like sparks. Generates it the way balloons generate static on your hair, the way picnics generate ants.

I ponder this as I trudge up the stairs, imagining lightning bolts of X flying from Matthew's fingertips. Each step seems more difficult than the one before, as if gravity is increasing the closer I get to the fifth floor. Which is, of course, impossible, since gravity decreases the farther you get from the center of the earth. But the laws of nature do not apply if the Dawg o' your dreams is waiting at a higher altitude, under the skylights of the fifth-floor lab, scrubbing out stinky rabbit hutches with a rag and totally, blissfully unaware of the BOMBSHELL OF LOVE you are about to drop upon his sweet head.

Still fortified by the strains of Kat's music playing in my mind's ear (and, for the record, she only had to stop once), I push open the door of the lab.

The stairwell is dim, but the lab is filled with light. On a sunny day like today, the room warms up and gets humid from all the plants growing under the skylights. I feel my pores opening up and hope the effect is more dewy glow than nervous perspiration. Either way, I'm here.

So is Matthew. Yellow rubber gloves, a red bandanna tied around his head to keep his hair off his face, a fat, silver-gray rabbit squirming under one arm.

"Hold Frosty a minute?" he says by way of greeting. I've never held Frosty before, but I know he's Matthew's favorite.

Like the genius rabbit he is, Frosty climbs happily into my arms, puts his two silver-tufted front paws on my chest, and touches his nose to mine. Matthew peels off his gloves and goes to wash his hands at the big utility sink by the back wall. Frosty gazes at me, all-knowing. These genius rabbits take some getting used to.

"Perfect timing. I'm ready for a break," Matthew

calls to me, drying his hands. He chats easily with his dozen or so mentally enhanced bunny friends, who are hopping loose around the lab. "You guys may be smart, but you sure are stinky."

Frosty is now snuffling my right ear. I wonder if he's trying to tell me something. Stop, before it's too late? Relax, everything will be fine? Or even, Don't worry, Matthew has been waiting for just this type of moment to confess his secret passion for you? Ha ha, very funny, superbunny.

I sit down on one of the wooden crates that are scattered around the room and do like Mom does during her morning meditation, which is supposed to make her all chilled out and wise and sagacious like the Dalai Lama (NOT! Aside to Mom: Can't you just take meds, like the other moms?). Breathe in, breathe out. Frosty seems to like the way my belly moves when I do this, and cuddles against me.

And then, it happens. I can't explain it, but somehow, everything seems different, safe, fundamentally okay on the molecular level. Frosty must be offering up some secret bunny mojo, the way Kat's violin does for her. The part of me that was freaking out seems to go *pfffft!* and fly away, and the part of me that's been aching to tell the truth starts to expand and grow lighter with every deep breath.

Frosty takes my thumb gently between his teeth and gives it an approving shake. Matthew returns and looks happy to see Frosty so contented in my lap.

Happy enough to decide he's actually madly, deeply, and X-cellently in love with me?

This Kitten is about to find out!

✗ ✗ ✗

Here's the part where I can pretend that Matthew heard me out, threw his arms around me and proposed, or at least asked me to the junior prom two years in advance. The Blissful End and fade out!

Or, here's the part where I can get all *Alice in Wonderland* and swear that Frosty actually leapt up between Matthew and me and spoke aloud, in a piping little bunny voice:

"Felicia! Matthew! My dear, sweet humans! How nice that you two, who are obviously and indisputably destined to be 2-gethah-4-evah, are finally discovering what we in the rabbit realm have always known! That the key to making happy burrows, which some call X, is quite simple, obvious really, but can only be attained by—Whoops! I'm late! I'm late!"

But that's not exactly what happens.

What does happen is this:

I look into Matthew's eyes, still feeling Frosty's encouraging teeth on my thumb, and I open my mouth, and out come words. They're clumsy, mumbled words that communicate, if you can make them out, some vague sense of an amazing phenomenon that demands to be understood, one of those ideas so self-evident that it's easy to miss, and clichés of that ilk.

"Cool," he says, unfazed by my idiocy. "What is it?"

"It's, uh, love," I hear myself say.

"Love. Whoa," says Matthew. "That's big."

"It is. That's why I want us to work as a team." My newborn voice is gaining some balance and starting to spread its folded, wet wings. "On their own, poets have only gotten so far on the subject of love, and they've

n that I will be working on a Very Special Science
roject this year, and with whom. She actually puts
nd on my forehead, like I'm sick or something.
agine and then we'll move on, because Matthew
ave a LOT of work to do. X is not going to reveal
ntity without a fight!

d I hope you enjoyed the poetic snippet above,
e that is the LAST poem you will be hearing from
: a while. I am a Scientist now. I even told Mr.
ni I was taking a break from writing poems till I
my New Perspective, though I will still drop by for
y Mister Mastor Mentor chats because we're pals.)
er cups of chai tea at the Moonbeam Diner,
ew explains to me that the scientific method has
steps:

Make observations.
Form a hypothesis based on your observations.
Make predictions based on your hypothesis.
Do experiments that test your predictions. If
hey work, you have discovered a Law of Nature
and can win valuable prizes! Dinner for two at
he Marriott, a convertible sophabed, or even
the Nobel!

, this is the sneaky, underhanded way they edu-
ou at the Pound. You think you're slacking off,
ng tea and mooning over Matthew in the
beam, but actually you're learning the scientific
d. Sneaky, sneaky.
r first step, make observations, means we must

mostly been describing the symptoms. And science, basically, is—"

"Primarily concerned with breeding," he mutters as
Frosty hops from my lap to his and starts chewing a but-
ton on his flannel shirt.

"Exactly." I can see that Matthew's mental wheels are
starting to spin. But before I can continue, he interjects.

"It's too broad a topic. It needs focus. A place to start."

"We start with me," I say simply.

"You?"

"Me. And you." Matthew sits up a little straighter,
now actually confused. Frosty starts climbing up his
chest and sits on his shoulder.

I lean forward. "Matthew, here's the thing."

Okay, here it comes, here's the thing. Breathe in,
breathe out. "I have a huge, huge crush on you. I have
for months." There, I said the thing. "And this crush I
have on you—it's really fascinating!" I choose my words
with care, working hard to keep this phenomenon of
ME BEING TOTALLY (OHMIGOD I'M TELLING
HIM!) IN LOVE WITH MATTHEW DWYER! in the
realm of scientific inquiry. "I mean, you're a great guy,
of course, any girl might reasonably have a crush on
you," I go on, reasonably. "But there are so many guys
at school! So why you? Why me? How does this type of
thing happen?"

Matthew's not screaming, or laughing, or running
away. My pal Frosty's nibbling on his hair, which I take
as a very good sign.

I build up to my big finish. "Based on the amount of
poetry, literature, art, and song that explores the nature
of love, I think a lot of people would be dying to get

some answers. Now," I conclude, with a touch of drama, "it's time for science to pick up the ball."

Matthew gently removes Frosty from the back of his neck and puts him on his lap, stroking his cloud-colored fur. He doesn't look at me at all, he just pets Frosty.

Who winks at me. (I swear, he really did.)

After ten eternal seconds of no sound at all but the contrapuntal breathing of Love-Struck Kitten, Bewildered Dawg, and Genius Rabbit, Matthew finally looks at me.

"I think we could win the science fair with this one" is what he says.

The Scientific Method
Action as Matthew and
Homework Assig

When Poet tries to correlate her Da
She picks a form of verse that won'
The Sonnets get iambic with her Th
Which hap'ly scans; she has no nee
Blank verse is best for the Hypothes
Because nothing rhymes with it.

Imagine, if you can, the Kittensh
alarm, rapidly giving way to amaz
say so!) grudging admiration, as I t
transpired under Frosty's watchful e

Imagine my mom's efforts not to

expla
Fair
her h

I
and
its id

(
beca
me f
Fras
foun
frien

C
Matt
seve

1
2
3
4

cate
drin
Mo
met

Observe the phenomenon we want to study and Describe what we see. I thought we could start with a basic review of the entire body of literature, poetry, and art pertaining to love since the beginning of time, just to get warmed up. But Matthew, insightfully, pointed out that this would take us probably the whole rest of our lives, and the science fair is in April. He also thinks it's best to focus on stuff that's actually happening in front of you, or that can be verified by primary sources (meaning the people who were there). See how smart my DeductiveDawg is?

As our mugs are refilled by one of the Moonies, we narrow down our fact-gathering objectives to the following list:

A: PRIMARY PHENOMENA OF LOVE
    • Felicia's crush on Matthew
    • Matthew's not-crush on Felicia
B: SECONDARY (AND HISTORIC) PHENOMENA OF LOVE, VERIFIED BY PRIMARY SOURCE INTERVIEWS WITH:
    • Our friends: Kat, Jess, Randall, Jacob
    • Our parents
    • Miscellaneous Wise and Cooperative
      Adults Who Might Have Something
      Interesting to Say About Love: Mr.
      Frasconi, et sweatera.

Jacob, by the way, is Matthew's other best Dawgbuddy besides Randall. Jacob is just getting back from Los Angeles, where his way-famous actress mom was opening in a play. Who knew they even had plays in Los Angeles?

Jacob is a bit mysterious but extremely well mannered, a deep Dawg with his own personal style. Jacob, get this, plans to be a professional sitar player one day.

Tea in mugs and list in hand, Matthew and I settle on some basic ground rules for our research.

We decide to conduct the interviews as a team, since one of us might unwittingly skip over stuff we already know about our Kitten- or Dawgpals or our own parents, and then the other one would not get to Observe and Describe the skipped-over stuff.

We decide to make Jacob our first interview subject, since he just got back from the Coast, baby, and Matthew wants to see him anyway and find out about his trip to La-La.

We also decide that, in order to maintain some secrecy about our project (ever since MIT, Microsoft, and NASA started sending talent scouts, the science fair at the Pound has been getting a bit competitive) and also because we are really loving this chai tea, we will have as many strategy meetings as possible here at the Moonbeam. We like this table, too, because of the way it catches the light at this late-afternoon hour and because it's not wobbly. We discuss the fact that we both hate wobbly diner tables.

And then, after a few moments of awkward silence, during which we each stir our sweet, spicy tea in slow circles and stare into the milky fortune-teller's swirls:

"So, I guess–" begins Matthew.

"–we should start–" I say, too quickly.

"With us. Like you said," he finishes. "You. And me."

And right then, our Moonie comes back with the check and we both look at her T-shirt and see the weird-shaped moon pictured there, and at the same time we say, as if we planned it but of course we didn't,

"Gibbous!"

And crack up so very hard.

Yet another reason why I'm CRAZY IN LOVE with Matthew Dwyer!

OBSERVATIONS AND DESCRIPTIONS OF
FELICIA'S CRUSH ON MATTHEW, OBSERVED
AND DESCRIBED BY ME, FELICIA!

When I think about Matthew I sometimes lose track of time and space. For example, I might become convinced that we are toasting marshmallows over a bonfire on the beach on a starry summer night, laughing at jokes that only we understand, when in reality I'm waiting on line at Duane Reade to pay for some contact lens fluid for my mom and Clearasil for me, and register three is open and I'm just standing there like a dork.

When I think there's a strong likelihood that I might see Matthew, I become urgently concerned with whether I have hat hair, and how my most recent meal may have affected my breath. Hat hair is not so much an issue in the warmer months, but breath is always with us.

When I'm around Matthew I often wish I were wearing something other than what I am wearing, though I don't know exactly what that might be. All my clothes are basically the same.

The most bizarre aspect of having a crush on

Matthew is how it makes even the most ordinary details about him seem unique and perfect. Generally speaking, all boys have hair, eyes, limbs, and speaking voices. Many have hobbies, at least some basic level of intelligence, and a rudimentary sense of humor. But seen through the adoring lens of my crush, Matthew's attributes in all these areas AND MORE are transformed into the Platonic Ideal of each, and I can accept No Substitutes!

The Platonic Ideal is a notion taken from Plato, that clever and ancient Greek, that there is basically a perfect version of everything floating somewhere in the big sky of human consciousness. I have just explained this to Matthew, who's better informed about bunny brains than he is about philosophy.

"Like Frosty is the Platonic Ideal of a rabbit," I add helpfully. Matthew looks over my essay again ("Felicia's Crush on Matthew," see above). His essay about me, still unread, lies on the park bench next to us. A fierce round of rock-paper-scissors determined that he would read mine first.

There were no tables at the diner, so we're in Madison Square Park, bundled in our coats and gloves, with take-out chais from Starbucks. Jacob will be joining us momentarily for his interview, and in the meantime we are exchanging the homework assignments we gave each other on Friday, before leaving the Moonbeam:

Felicia, Observe and Describe Your Crush on Matthew.
Matthew, Observe and Describe Your Not-Crush on Felicia.

Somewhere in the difference between the two, we feel, we will start to pick up the trail of X.

Matthew peruses my essay with a frowny, serious expression. "Your clothes are fine," he says abruptly.

"I know! It's irrational," I say. "That's the whole point." We each sip our tea. Gluttonous, multicolored pigeons are pecking away at the crumbled saltines somebody threw on the ground in front of our bench.

"And I wouldn't even notice if you had hat hair."

"Matthew," I say, sensing his cluelessness. "Haven't you ever had a crush? It makes your mind do strange things."

"I can see that," he agrees, looking at the paper. "Temporal and spatial disorientation, heightened sensitivity and self-consciousness. Distorted judgment." He winces. "Is it painful? It sounds pretty unpleasant."

The pigeons suddenly take off with a coordinated flopping of their semi-useless wings as Jacob skids to a stop on his Razor scooter right in front of us.

"Matthew, dude!" he exclaims. Jacob is always blond, but now he's really tan and his hair is bleached platinum by the sun and ratted into little funky-white-boy dreads. "And gracious greetings to the Lady Poet." He bows to me, medieval-courtier style.

"Nice melanin production, Jake," says Matthew, standing up and giving Jacob one of those back-slapping guy hugs where they bump chests but their faces never get near each other. "How was the trip?"

"Oh, dude, my sweet mama is such a nutcase when she's opening a new show. I pity her anxiety. Whoops, apologies, Mr. Cracker!" He's just stepped on the last of the saltines. "It was cool hanging out on the beach, though, playing my sitar. The good people of La-La were totally appreciative."

"That's nice," I say.

"It's because their spirits are all malnourished from the filthy air and soulless Hollywood vibe," Jacob says, smacking his arms to keep warm. "You guys wanna go on the swings?"

We gather our 'bucks cups and our backpacks. I take special care to slide Matthew's essay into a safe spot in my notebook so it doesn't get crumpled.

There's a small playground at the uptown end of Madison Square Park. Unlike us Free Teenage Children of the Pound, who can wander wherever we like as long as it's relevant to our project du jour, the little kids are locked up in classrooms during the day, daring each other to eat paste and learning how to fold cootie catchers. So we'll have the swings all to ourselves.

Jacob is a virtuoso of the Razor scooter, doing hairpin turns and popping ollies and weaving in between horrified senior citizens at incredible speed. He circles and swerves around me and Matthew as the three of us head toward the swings. This makes his voice cut in and out, so I can't hear all of what he's saying.

"You should swear off the 'bucks, man—*something*—the mallification of America—*something something*—corporate java mind control—*something something something*—a caffeine-laden tool for global domination— Oh, this is cool, people. Watch this."

Jacob accelerates on his scooter and jumps off it directly onto a swing, landing on his belly and arcing through the air as the confused Razor crash-lands against the fence.

He flips over onto his butt and starts whooping and pumping his legs and having a grand old time. It seems the only way we're going to get any interview material from Jacob is to take to the air. Swings make me queasy, but science is not for wusses, as I'm beginning to learn.

It takes a while to calibrate our swinging so we're all moving forward and backward in unison.

"So, Jacob!" I yell. "What's your experience of love?"

"I love New York, baby!" he crows.

"That's great, buddy," shouts Matthew. "But we mean love, love. Romantic love, FM-radio-love-song love."

"You mean love with chicks?" Jacob says as we all pump our legs.

"Sure! If that's the way you swing!" Matthew says, making us snort with laughter.

"There was this one girl," yells Jacob. "She was it for me, I mean IT. I will never, ever"—we're all getting breathless now—"ever, find someone as perfect as her."

"Who, man? You never mentioned a girl," says Matthew.

Jacob stops pumping, so we do, too. "She was riding the L train," he says, sounding wistful. "I watched her put on her lip gloss all the way from Lorimer Street to Eighth Avenue, even though I was supposed to change at Union Square." We're slowing down, down, down. "Then she got off the train. She was wearing orange sneakers. I will never see her like again."

"When was this?" I ask, trying not to sound suspicious. Frankly, I am not sure this qualifies as a Love Phenomenon. And that seems like quite a lot of lip gloss.

"Seventh grade. Ah, the folly of youth." Jacob seems genuinely sad.

"Could be time to move on, bro," says Matthew, not unkindly.

"No doubt, no doubt." Jacob has stopped swinging and scuffs the ground with his big Great Dane–puppy feet. "Loving the wrong woman can lead to calamity, for sure. You should see the play my mom's in. She gets peeved at her ex and like, burns his new wife to a crisp with acid, and then, like that's not enough mayhem, she grabs a knife and utterly Tarantinos these two little kids they had together. It's a gorefest, man. It's mad violent."

"That's tragic," says Matthew.

"That's *Medea,*" I say.

"Exactly," Jacob says. "Only with TV screens and stuff. It's a modern version. Mother Thespian got some excellent reviews. The dude from *Variety* thought she had 'ferocious clarity.' "

We all agree that having ferocious clarity sounds extremely cool, as Jacob retrieves his scooter.

"Sorry I couldn't be more, whatever," says Jacob. "But I applaud the wild and unrealistic ambition of your project."

"And, hey, sorry about the L train girl," says Matthew. "It's a loss. But you'll survive."

"No, Mattski," says Jacob, suddenly quite serious. "Think Eastern for a minute. It's not the loss that leads to suffering. It's ego, man. It's the fact that Miss Orange Sneakers did not even notice me falling in love with her. To me, during those like, twelve precious minutes we were in each other's lives, she was the, what is that expression? The crème de la plooz, you know, the people's choice, the best of the best."

"Ne plus ultra," I fill in.

"Right. But to her, I was just another nameless face

on the L train. If she even saw me. I gotta live with that, you know, *ordinariness.* That's painful."

Matthew looks at me. "Oh," he says. "Is *that* the painful part?"

I nod, while thinking to myself that Jacob is certainly far from ordinary. "Yup," I say. "That's pretty much it."

Jacob is rocking back and forth on the Razor, balancing first on one wheel, then the other. "Oh, hey!" he says. "You should talk to Dervish. She's done her time in the big house of love, to be sure."

"Who's Dervish?" I ask.

"Miss Greenstream. My sitar teacher. She's a way highly evolved soul. Come any Saturday, after my lesson." Jacob does a fast one-eighty on the back wheel of his scooter.

"Peace, people! I wish you—ferocious clarity!" He pounds his fist in the air as he zooms off. "Whoo-hooooo!"

OBSERVATIONS AND DESCRIPTION:
MATTHEW DWYER'S NOT-CRUSH ON FELICIA

I would like to note that from a scientific standpoint, it is unusual to observe a phenomenon by describing its absense. [sic—okay, he's not the greatest speller—F.]

I cannot say that I have a "crush," or any other "romantic" feelings for Felicia. However, I do like her very much and find her interesting and intelligent, with a good sense of humor. I consider her a friend. She is a perfectly pleasant-looking person and I find no single aspect of her off-putting in any way.

To tell the truth, the feelings commonly referred to as a "crush"—a heightened interest in one particular person, a sense of longing for that person's company and affection, and even a level of anxiety regarding whether the "crush" feeling is returned—although I understand these sensations intellectually, I don't really have direct experience—

"Ready for lights-out, honey?" Mom is standing in the doorway of my bedroom with her hand on the switch.

"Matthew finds no single aspect of me offputting in any way," I tell her. "That's good, isn't it?"

"Wellllllllll, it's not baaaaaad," she replies, with a singsongy tune in her voice. She presses her lips together in that way people inexplicably call pursed. "Honey," she croons, "you don't think that by doing this project with Matthew you're going to change the way he feels, do you? Because that would be the wrong reason to do it—"

Motherdear, who thinks she's so smart. "No!" I say, in hot denial. "We're friends now. We're gonna blow the lid off the science fair, that's all."

"Well, I think it's very open of you to share your feelings with him." Note Motherdear's use of the *O* word. "And Matthew must be a very open person to hear your feelings without freaking out," she continues, hammering her point. "So obviously you have good taste!"

At this, I must have started to look, I don't know, sad or something, because in a jiffy Mom was sitting on the bed next to me rubbing my back, like she used to do every night when I was little. "Sweetie pie, remember that boys at fourteen can be much less mature than girls at fourteen." She drones on, randomly spewing overused Momisms: "Everybody grows up in their own time. . . . many fish in the sea . . . blah blah blah . . ."

Yeah, right. And nobody spends the rest of her life INSANELY in love with her freshman-year crush. Till now, that is.

—although I understand these sensations intellectually, I don't really have direct experience—

How could someone who gives off so much X not know what love feels like? As Mom prattles, I feel the needle on my inner dubiosity meter twitching into the red zone.

That's never a good sign.

5

I Discover Who Loves Me in a Place
I Have No Business Being

I have never seen Jess looking as determined as she does right now. And that is saying something.

"The teachers talk and talk, and most of the class is not even LISTENING. Three—THREE!—out of thirty-four students in the English class turned in their homework on time. At least Doris Jean Amberson was one of them," she says with a sigh.

Jess and Kat and I have gathered for our weekly mathfest in the fourth-floor math room. We find that doing math once a week for an entire Krispy Kreme–fueled morning works better than doing it every day for a shorter length of time. This way it doesn't get boring, and we surely do look forward to the donuts.

Kat is by far the most Komputational Kitten among us, so she generally leads the way, mathwise, but Ms. Blank is nearby if we need help. Ms. Blank is the Pound's Math Mentor. At the moment Ms. Blank is lying on the floor. Her left hand is on her forehead, shielding her eyes, and her right hand is writing something invisible in the air. It looks like she's conducting an orchestra while suffering from a migraine, but we know she's actually trying to memorize the value of pi to a thousand places. It's sort of a hobby of hers.

Jess's two weeks of peer tutoring with D. J. Amberson have not gone well. "She won't let me help her at all!" Jess reported after their third session. "She sits there and does her homework, and if I offer a suggestion she just looks over her shoulder like she's afraid someone will see us talking. I WISH I knew what was going on!" By yesterday, Jess had resolved to take matters into her own tiny, iron hands.

"I just showed up at her school yesterday morning and tagged along. Look." Jess shows us her binder, which now has a tab clearly labeled "A Day in the Life of D.J." "I started with homeroom and stayed with her every period. English, social studies, math, gym, lunch, biology, study hall. WHAT an interesting experience!"

Kat and I both have donut sugar all over the lower halves of our faces (Kitten Directive Number Eighteen: Neatness Among Kittenpals Is NOT Required!). We listen, our mouths crammed full of glazed chocolate (me) and jelly-filled (Kat).

"First, EVERYBODY calls her Deej, which she never told me. Second, she spends most of the day trying not to get into fights." Jess is wide-eyed. "I mean, FISTfights! One girl in her class has a scar on her cheek where some other girl SLASHED her with an umbrella!"

"Excuse me," Ms. Blank is speaking from the floor, her eyes still closed.

"Sorry, Ms. B," I say. Jess has been getting kind of loud.

"French," says Ms. B slowly. We wait for the rest. "Cruller," she finishes thoughtfully.

Ms. B's hand pauses in the air long enough to take a cruller from Kat, who's sitting closest. "But get this," continues Jess, choosing the last Boston cream and holding it delicately between two fingers. "She SINGS."

"Sings what?" asks Kat, her interest piqued by the conversation's sudden veer toward the topic of music.

"All kinds of stuff. During lunch, Deej and these two other girls—one of them was named Shelly, I think—they went into the corner of the parking lot—which is where they have recess, by the way, between the CARS!—and they sang. In harmony! They were just having fun, but Deej is really good."

"Did they mind you listening?" I ask. Having Jess follow me around scribbling notes in her All-Knowing Binder would be a little trying, and she's my pal and littermate. I'm afraid to imagine how Deej and her friends felt about it.

"You could say that," says Jess brightly. I notice for the first time that both of Jess's knees are scraped, but before I can ask about it the door of the math room opens, thus permitting (insert Strutting HottieBoy Music here)—

The Entrance of Dawgs!

But it's only Randall. He's our next Search for X interview, purely by the luck of the draw. I don't expect that Randall will have anything illuminating to say about the workings of passion, but he's Matthew's friend and he's on our list, so here he is.

To be fair, there's no single aspect of Randall that's off-putting in any way (ha ha, couldn't resist!). He has good posture, I'll give him that. In his extra-Poundicular life, Randall trains and competes in some martial arts discipline or other. Supposedly, he whups ass. It's kind of hard to picture.

"Hey," he says, spotting us. Nope, Randall does not sound like he even remotely has ass-whupping capabilities. "Hey, Ms. Blank."

Ms. Blank's air-doodling briefly takes the form of a wave. Randall slides into an empty seat at our table. He lifts the lid of the donut box and peers inside.

"Have one," I offer.

But Randall quickly shakes his head. "I don't think my sensei would consider this 'eating to win,' " he says.

"I consider it 'eating to eat,' " I riposte. (A riposte is a snappy comeback. How like the French to invent a word that means snappy comeback.)

Randall does not offer a riposte to my riposte, nor does he even look at me. Instead, he blushes a faint shade of pink and turns to Kat. "How's the practicing going?" he asks.

It's not unusual for Dawgs to get Tunnel-KatVision when we're all hanging out together. Kat does nothing to encourage this, which only makes it more obvious. But outwardly speaking, Kat is on the tall and skinny side of the spectrum, and has this kind of Russian look to her, since her parents are both Russian (her mother, in fact, still lives in Moscow, a source of much sadness to our lonelyKitten Kat!). She has broad cheekbones and nearly almond-shaped, golden-brown eyes, with a swishy mane of straight, buttery-blond hair that she lets hang in her face most of the time. Total effect: chilled teen supermodel with a twist of mystery, and Dawgs do love a Secretive Kat!

"Practicing's fine," she says inaudibly. Randall nods. They both seem satisfied with this conversation. I wonder, fleetingly, if Randall and Kat would make a good, if largely silent, couple. Can X be summoned in this way? Or does it have to show up on its own?

"Well! I FINALLY feel like I have a handle on those polynomials," announces Jess as she pulls her frizzy hair into a knot on top of her head and turns to me. "NOW we can help with your science project!"

At this, Randall looks even paler than usual. "Yeah, I wanted to talk to you about that– Um, where's Matthew?"

I glance up. The fourth-floor math room is directly underneath the lab, where Matthew communes with his brilliant bunnies. "Upstairs," I say. "He'll be here."

Randall looks up, too, as if Matthew is going to burst through the plaster. He starts to mumble. "See, it turns out I have, like, a lot of stuff to do today. . . ." His voice trails off.

"Don't freak out, Randall," I say, trying to sound reassuring. "We just have a few really, really personal questions to ask you!" I laugh, to lighten things up, but it doesn't seem to work. Randall fidgets. There are candy sprinkles scattered all over the table from the donuts. Randall starts to sort them by color into anxious little piles.

That's when Matthew arrives (through the door, not the ceiling). My tummy gives its customary Matthew-is-in-the-room lurch, and I uselessly run my hand through my hair to fluff it, Meg Ryan style.

Matthew's not alone, though.

"Yo-YO, it's the Randinator and his harem! Gimme some skin, O lethal one!" The Randinator high-fives Trip with a pathetic lack of gusto, knocking his neat sprinkle piles everywhere.

Trip is not your average student at the Pound, not that there is such a thing. Trip's name is really Harold or Harcourt or some prehistorically old-money family name like that, but whatever it is he's the third one, so his nickname's been Trip since he was a babe in his nanny's hired arms. He's gone to boarding school in Switzerland, three different private schools uptown, and even (rumor has it) some kind of youth rehab place. Now he's basically chillin' at the Pound, technically a freshman but sixteen years old due to his Lost Years.

"Howdy, pardner!" Matthew gives me a half-smile and an actual who's-your-buddy? PUNCH on the arm. How romantic. "You will never believe what we just did!"

"Psychic rabbits, people! Matthew is da man!" Trip seems to be able to talk about one thing with his mouth and say something completely different with his eyes. Right now he's looking at Kat, and his eyes are talking a mile a minute.

"Psychic RABBITS?" says Jess. Jess is not even fully

convinced that *people* can be psychic. We've had long debates about this.

"Trip concentrated on an image, and the rabbits had to guess which one by pushing a lever," explains Matthew. "Not all of them showed psychic aptitude, but Frosty, Fluffy, and George scored well above what could be predicted by chance."

Trip angles himself toward Kat. "These bunnies were *reading my mind,*" he says to her meaningfully. How cool, Trip, like we're not all reading your mind right now! Kat scoots her chair back a little and glances at Jess and me for help.

"Did it work both ways?" I ask innocently. "Did you develop a craving for carrots at any point?"

"Totally," laughs Trip. "Now I know exactly what bunnies think about." He looks at Kat, laying on that rich-boy charm. "And they think about it all the time!"

"Rabbits actually prefer lettuce," Matthew says to me.

An image forms in my mind, of me and Matthew walking down the aisle to the strains of the wedding march. *Ba-dum-de-dum!* Big fat happy rabbits hop around our feet. The rabbits wear bow ties. I am carrying a beautiful bouquet of iceberg lettuce. . . .

"Listen," says Randall. Practically invisible, see? I almost forgot he was here. "I have to go. Really sorry, guys."

"What about our interview, bud? Won't take long at all," says Matthew, who apparently sees nothing unusual in Randall's demeanor.

"Yeah, can't do it. Just so much going on today. Sorry!"

Matthew looks at me. I shrug. No great loss, in my

opinion. "Okay, maybe we can reschedule," says Matthew affably. "And we have a brief questionnaire, you can fill it out at home. Only takes a few minutes."

"Sure, that's what I'll do." It seems to me that Randall might really be blushing now, but he grabs the questionnaire from Matthew and hustles out of the math room so fast I can't tell. I wonder briefly what would make the Randinator and his Fists of Fire beat such a hasty retreat. I am not alone in my wondering.

"Whence the embarrassment?" asks Trip as soon as Randall's gone. "You taking a survey about STDs?" Despite his former brain-frying exploits, Trip doesn't seem to miss much.

"Felicia and I are collecting data for our science fair project," says Matthew, eyeing the Krispy Kreme box with the kind of longing he seems not to feel for humans—at least, not THIS human. I push the box toward him with my best come-hither smile, but then I remember I probably have chocolate on my teeth.

Trip looks at me for the first time. "Working as a team, huh? Sweet." I feel him wondering why on earth Matthew would be doing a science project with me. "What's it about?"

"Strictly confidential." I smirk.

"Unless, of course, you'd be willing to answer a few questions," says Matthew through his donut. "Randall split," he says, turning to me. "And data is data."

Spoken like a scientist! Trip leans back, balancing his chair on two legs. "A gentleman never discusses money, politics, or religion. So sayeth Junior." (It takes me a mathematical minute to figure out that Junior must be

Trip's dad.) Trip laughs. "But I'm not much of a gentleman, so fire away! The old man keeps me on a pretty short leash these days, so answering questions is what I do best."

I can't help thinking that Trip is not the spoiled thug I expected him to be. At least, not entirely.

"What about you beauties?" Trips says, turning to Jess and Kat. "Are you being interrogated, too?"

Kat peers at Trip through her hair. "Yes," she says eloquently.

"It's Felicia and Matthew's project. But of course we've agreed to be interviewed," says Jess.

"Excellent! We can bare our souls together. But I am so sick of being indoors," Trip says, to me this time. "Why don't you gather up your questionnaires and your number two pencils and your truth serum, and we'll go pay a visit to Gram?"

The donuts were gone, and Ms. Blank was now snoring ever so quietly on the floor. Clearly, there would be no more math today. A visit to Gram sounded perfect. More importantly, we could get three interviews done in one afternoon! As Matthew is fond of saying, data is our friend.

And that is how, a short while later, Matthew, Trip, Jess, Kat, and I found ourselves breaking in to Gramercy Park.

Gramercy Park is what they call a key park, meaning you need a key to get in, and it's the only key park left in New York City. Perhaps this sounds snobbish, but private, padlocked, *Secret-Garden*esque Gramercy Park is the last of its breed, and I for one would hate to see the black iron gates torn down. Gram wouldn't feel quite as magical inside if it weren't somehow forbidden.

To have a key to the park, you have to live in one of the buildings surrounding it. The Pound has a key, but its use is strictly monitored and involves filling out an application and having it signed by a faculty member. When I was struggling with the seasonal reference conundrum in my haiku phase, Mr. Frasconi approved me for Gram visits at least once a week, so I could "observe nature and respond in poetry, dreams, or personal reflection." Mr. Frasconi's coolness knows no bounds.

Keyless—that is to say, rule-breaking—drop-ins to Gram are not unheard of, especially among the older Free Children, but I personally have never done it and am experiencing an emotional cocktail of one part rebelgrrl, twelve parts wussypants, and forty thousand parts don't-act-like-a-dumb-wussypants-in-front-of-Matthew. Trip leads us to the corner farthest from the Pound, where Gramercy Park East meets East Twentieth Street. A large tree with a low, overhanging branch reaches through the fence in a way that can only be called inviting.

Trip pulls himself up onto the branch. From where he's perched it's a short step up to the top rail of the iron fence.

"Who's first?" says Trip. He extends his hand, and before you can say "nerves of steel," Jess is on the branch next to him. She flashes me a big, adventure-loving grin before taking the leap. There's a soft thud.

"Oooooooooh," coos Jess's voice from inside the park. "It's SO beautiful!"

Kat flies up next, her lean arms strong from countless hours with the violin. "Let me go first so I can catch you," offers Trip, the very model of Dawg-on-the-make gallantry. He hops effortlessly over the fence. Kat follows, landing with a giggle. A giggle! From Kat!

"Hey, you're light as a feather," I hear Trip's voice say.

Now it's just me and Matthew, the intrepid investigators of *amour*. "After you," he says, smiling that irresistibly inscrutable Matthew Dwyer half-smile. He laces his fingers together so I can use his hands to step up to the branch.

It's always so nice to be in a tree, I think, before realizing I've said it out loud.

"Yes, it is," agrees Matthew. He's next to me on the branch now. We can peer over the fence and the thick evergreen hedge and see almost all of the little private wooded park. I know Gram well from ground level, but this is a brand-new vantage point.

Matthew and Felicia sittin' in a tree, *K-I-S-S-I-N-G*! Who writes these songs?

Matthew holds out his hand, and I take it, and together we jump over the fence, landing butt-first on a hard, damp pile of wood chips.

(Felicia's Private Kitten Directive Number Ohmigod-Matthew-Held-My-Hand!: All Instances of Matthew-Felicia Body Contact MUST be Logged in Felicia's Notebook Within Twenty-Four Hours of Occurring!)

Trip, Jess, and Kat are standing there smiling, covered with bits of bark and dead leaves.

"You guys look like garden gnomes," says Matthew, laughing. Trip hunkers down and makes comical gnome-like movements. Kat struggles not to smile and fails. We start to walk along the gravelly path.

The past sunny week has deslushified the ground,

leaving only the glittering remains of melting icicles dripping off the tree branches. Now that it's March, little nubs of green crocus tips are pushing up through the dirt, right on schedule.

"All right," says Matthew as we walk. "We have a few basic questions for all of you. First: What is your experience of love?"

"Whoa there, youngstah!" Trip exclaims, turning around. "What do you mean? Second base, third base, all the way?"

"He said *love*. Not *baseball*," says Kat, with the tiniest shade of Violin Kat edge in her voice.

"It's all sport, beautiful Katarina!" says Trip, throwing his arms wide. "A competition, with winners and losers. And some lucky dude takes home the gold medal! All shiny and golden, just like your pretty hair."

"That's fascinating, Trip," I say. "But what we really need to know is, have you ever been in love?"

"And if so," Matthew continues, "what qualities in the environment, or circumstances of meeting, or in the actual object of your affection—"

"—meaning, the person you fell in love with," I add, to clarify.

"—right, which of those factors caused or contributed to the actual 'falling in love' experience?" asks Matthew.

"And," I go on, "if there was a subsequent 'falling out of love' experience, exactly what change may have occurred in said environment or circumstances—"

"—or object of your affection—" says Matthew.

"—right, to precipitate that happening?" Whew! Matthew and I high-five. We are good at this.

Trip and Kat and Jess are staring at us like three

bobble-heads from those quarter vending machines, trying to keep up.

"You know," says Jess, "I'm NOT being critical, but that is actually kind of complicated."

"But they're asking about *love*," says Kat. "Love *is* complicated. People do terrible things for love." This is the sort of thing her dad often tells her. I feel the Russian melancholy wafting in, pooling like fog around her feet.

"You crazy kids today," says Trip. "When I was fourteen we didn't care about love. We just wanted to make out!"

We're approaching the center of lovely Gram. There are few people here besides us: an overdressed woman with her overdressed dogs, a businessman in a trench coat talking on his cell phone. There is someone who's always here, though, and as we reach the central circle he looms in front of us, black and imposing and always just about to speak. It's the statue of Edwin Booth.

Edwin Booth, says the plaque at the base of the statue, was the greatest American Shakespearean actor of the nineteenth century. He was also the brother of John Wilkes Booth, a less talented actor who ended up far more famous than Edwin because he assassinated Abraham Lincoln. However, I don't think there are any statues of John Wilkes Booth in New York City or elsewhere, so the moral is, it pays to come by your fame honestly.

"Let's cut to the chase here," says Trip as we reach the statue. "What is this project? What is it that you kids wanna know?"

"To BE, or NOT to BE?" replies Edwin Booth, with

really impressive diction. But I think I imagined it. I mean, duh, of course I imagined it.

"The secret of love," Matthew says.

"Why some combinations of people fall in love, and others don't," I explain.

"It was Felicia's idea," Matthew adds helpfully.

Trip turns to me. "And how much Canadian hydroponic monster weed did you smoke to come up with this notion?" he asks, sounding more friendly-teasing than mean-teasing.

It occurs to me that I'm going to have to explain this over and over again should we actually make it to the science fair, so I might as well get thick-skinned about it. "Well, I've had this big crush on Matthew since, like, September," I begin oh-so-casually. "And it made me wonder what exactly is the reason for things like that happening."

"You devil!" Trip smacks Matthew on the arm.

"People sometimes call it chemistry. We're calling it X, since we don't know what it is."

"Yet," Matthew adds.

Trip looks at me with a fresh appreciation that seems totally genuine. "That's fearless," he says. "I think you are the coolest chick I ever met."

"That's because she IS," says Jess, hugging me fiercely. Kat nods her endorsement. Is Matthew getting all this? I look at him, but he has his scientist face on.

"Bummer that we lost Randall, though," Matthew says. "We sure could use the data points. I wonder what's up?"

Trip snorts, the ways of the world so obvious to him. "Read the writing on the wall, people!" he says, striking the same dramatic pose as Mr. Edwin Booth, Shakespearean Actor! "Randall doesn't want to answer your probing questions about love because he's *in* love! And I think it's with the Marie Curie of romance here!"

It takes me a minute to realize he means me.

Now everyone is looking at me. Even Edwin Booth is looking at me.

Me! You know, the coolest chick ever?

Love *objet* of the Randinator?

ME????

6

Two Brownstones, Two Interviews, Too Much Information!

As their wanderlust reaches critical, a conga line of photons say *"¡Mañana!"* to the sun and go partying across the solar system till they hit the Earth's atmosphere, curving ever so slightly before whooshing across the Pacific Ocean; then California, the Rocky Mountains, and the flat Midwest to fragrant New Jersey; they skitter across the Hudson River, wait impatiently for the light to change on Broadway, and, finally losing speed, slant through the west-facing windows of the Moonbeam Diner to make strange, late-afternoon patterns of light and shadow on our table as Matthew and I sip chai tea and review what we've learned from our interviews so far.

For one thing, we're ditching the questionnaire. When it comes to love, multiple choice does not cut it.

Also, we concede that the Kittens and Dawgs, much as we worship them, have disappointingly little useful data to offer about love. To wit:

Jacob: The L-train girl. 'Nuff said.

Trip: Sees a girl, falls in love. Five minutes later the feeling's gone and he's on to the next girl. He has no explanation for this and suspects it's related to his ADD. ("But you can get into a LOT of trouble in five minutes!" he chortled.)

The Randall-Loves-Me Thing: *Sacre bleu!* Too much for my Kittenbrain to process, not to mention this is the last thing I want to sit here discussing with Matthew! Both of us have tactfully neglected to bring it up.

(By the way, Randall turned in a completely bogus questionnaire, filled with insightful responses like "No comment" and "I don't know." However, in the part where we ask for suggestions of other people to interview, he put down that we should meet with his sensei— that's his martial arts instructor. Matthew and I agree that this sounds intriguing. So now, in addition to our parents, the Miscellaneous Adults list includes Randall's sensei, Mr. Frasconi, and Miss Dervish Greenstream, sitar teacher to the stars.)

Jess: She hung out with a boy from her synagogue briefly last year, but it was mostly a by-product of the peace rally she was organizing. Once the posters were finished they didn't have much in common. She also admitted to warm feelings of admiration for Gandhi and a true schoolgirl crush on Mr. Rochester, that brooding, tormented stud-muffin from *Jane Eyre*, but Gandhi is dead and Mr. Rochester is fictional, so that's not too helpful.

Kat: As expected, Kat claimed to steer clear of Dawg action, because of her music-mindedness and also because her dad has no intention of allowing her to date till she's like, thirty. However, after much flirtatious prodding from Trip she confided that there's some weird vibe going on with her new accompanist, Dmitri, a gross old guy who is giving her the creeps. More news as it develops!

And don't forget Matthew and his pal, his pardner, his ol' buddy, me. Felicia. Insert a Sigh of Unbearable Frustration HERE.

And that is the Moonbeam roundup. We are hoping our interviews with the grownups will provide juicier material. Without some specifics it's going to be hard to design our experiments, which Matthew says is our next task.

"Based on your observations, you might notice, say, that plants seem to need light to grow. That's your hypothesis. But now you have to prove it. So you design an experiment where one plant is in the light and one plant is in the dark, and you chart their growth, keeping all other variables the same, and soon you have lots and lots of data! And that's doing science!" Matthew is never so happy as when he's explaining something tedious like this to me. But I don't mind. I watch the way his lips move over his teeth as he talks. I wonder if he's more of a wet kisser or a dry one? I wonder if he's ever kissed anybody who wasn't a rabbit? Would that I could find out!

Matthew goes to pay for our chais at the cash register, leaving me alone for some private pondering. It's pretty easy to see when X is in the room, but what the *borscht* is it? Some thoughts:

I can see that Trip definitely gives off X, but not the kind that would work on me, for instance.

And it's obvious that Kat has the kind of X that works on many Dawgs, like Trip, for example, but if it only lasts five minutes then it's not really X, is it?

And, okay. This business about ME having X, except it's only visible to Randall's bespectacled eyes? That makes no sense. How could I give off X for Randall but not for Matthew, when Matthew is the Dawg of Dawgs, my soul mate of soul mates?

Earlier, after we left Gram (through the gate this time, moseying out after the cell phone/trenchcoat/business-man guy with a key, who gave us quite the dirty look) and the Kittens and Dawgs went our separate ways, I asked Kat and Jess what they thought of Trip's insane proclamation that Randall was in love with me. I mean, Randall? Please.

"Oh my GOD! I can't believe I didn't notice it before!" exclaimed Jess. "Randall is ALWAYS so nervous around you! It explains a LOT."

"But, but but—" I sputtered. "But RANDALL?"

"He's very smart. And not a show-off, like other boys," murmured Kat. Was she thinking of Trip?

"And he's CUTE! But of course, you're SO not interested! I mean, you're in love with Matthew. So put it OUT of your mind!" said Jess, neatly solving this problem, as she does all others.

Oh! It was my turn to look like a cartoon of a surprised person. Did my Kittenpals think Trip was right?

And do they actually consider Randall to be potential LovahDawg material?

I mean, please! RANDALL?

Randall's X is obviously misfiring, that's the explanation. His signals are getting crossed and confusing everyone. Or maybe Trip really is a spoiled thug and was teasing me, and the Kittens are mistaken. It could happen.

I decide to follow Jess's advice and put the whole Randall thing out of my mind, which is already TOO FULL! With thoughts of Matthew, of course. Now that we're spending so much time together, the flame under my krazy Kittencrush has been turned up, up, up. What was a steamy simmer is now a constant, rolling boil. Not that he's given me the least sign of encouragement. He doesn't have to. He's Matthew Dwyer, and that seems to be all it takes to put my X-receptors into overdrive.

"Hello!" Mrs. Dwyer says brightly when I arrive at Matthew's apartment—whoops, I mean house, in Park Slope, Brooklyn, on Friday evening. I had suggested we interview *Mère* and *Père* Dwyer together at a time when his dad would be home from work, and Matthew, though a bit lacking in enthusiasm, agreed.

"You must be Matthew's friend! Come in!" she titters. Brownstone houses in Park Slope, for those who do not know about these things, are nice, very nice, MUCH nicer than where my mom and I live. I start to kick off my shoes, because we never wear shoes inside at home, but then I see that Mrs. Dwyer is in a pair of beige pumps. When in Rome, keep your shoes on.

"Matty!" his mom sings out. "Your friend is here!"

She walks backward into the dining room, smiling at me, making little follow-me gestures with her hands. I follow.

There's a tray already set out on the huge mahogany table, with a silver pitcher of juice and three glasses.

"What a nice home you have," I say.

"Yes," she agrees, pouring me some juice. "Do you and your parents live in Park Slope? It's such a lovely neighborhood!"

"No, my mom and I live in the East Village," I say. She's looking at me in a funny, intense way. "And my dad lives in New Jersey."

Her smile takes on a twist of sympathy, but whether in response to the divorced parents or New Jersey I can't tell.

Matthew appears in the doorway. He looks damp, like he just got out of the shower. "Hey," he says. "Mom, this is Felicia."

"What a lovely name," Mrs. Dwyer says. She keeps looking at me. I wonder if I've got bird poop in my hair or something.

"Where's Dad?" says Matthew.

"Oh!" says Mrs. Dwyer. "He had to work late."

"Right," Matthew says. "We should get started, then."

"There's no rush, Matty!" says Mrs. Dwyer. "I like chatting with your friend." She takes a huge, heavy photo album off one of the bookshelves and hands it to me just as I'm about to sip my juice. I put my glass down so I can hold the album.

"Mom—" Matthew says, sounding annoyed.

Mrs. Dwyer ignores him. "You might enjoy seeing these!" she says to me. I flip open the book. Baby pictures! I'd recognize Matthew anywhere.

"Bald as an egg till he was three," Mrs. Dwyer confides. I flip the pages forward. Now Matthew is in kindergarten. He's holding a trophy that's nearly as tall as he is.

"Such a serious little face," she says. "And he won! Imagine his face if he'd lost! But Matthew always won."

"We just have a few simple questions," Matthew mumbles to the table.

"So how do you like the MFCS?" Mrs. Dwyer asks me. "We think it's such a lovely, progressive school. I wish Matty would tell us more about what goes on there!"

"Can we get this over with?" says Matthew.

The phone rings. Matthew pops up like a piece of toast and scurries out of the room to grab it. Mrs. Dwyer is still smiling at me. "So how long have you and Matthew been . . . friends?"

"Oh, six months, I guess," I say. "Since school started, more or less."

"REALLY?" she says, as if this were important news. "Would you like some strudel?" she offers.

In a flash, I realize: she thinks I'm Matthew's girlfriend.

But how bizarro is that? I mean, if I were Matthew's girlfriend, for six months, wouldn't she have met me before? And didn't Matthew tell her about our science project?

Matthew comes back into the room. "It was Jacob. Our meeting with Miss Greenstream is confirmed for tomorrow. He gave me the address. One o'clock, right after his lesson."

"Great," I say.

"Miss Greenstream? Is she a teacher at school?" asks

Mrs. Dwyer. She's still smiling, but it's starting to look a little strained.

"She's Jacob's sitar teacher," I say.

"Who's Jacob?" she asks.

"A kid at school," says Matthew blandly. "We have to ask a few questions about you and Dad."

"How come you never bring your friends over?" says Mrs. Dwyer to Matthew.

"We would love to know how you and Mr. Dwyer met!" I chime in.

"Oh, such a long time ago! I can barely remember," giggles Mrs. Dwyer, though it's not clear what's funny. "It was at work. Matthew's father and I used to work together."

Data! At last! I decide to press ahead. "Would you say it was love at first sight?"

"More like forbidden fruit!" She giggles again, nervously. "The grass is always greener, something like that."

I'm not following this. "Why was it forbidden? Because you worked together?"

"My dad was married before," says Matthew to me. He turns to his mom. "So you mean he was still married, when you–"

"Such a long time ago," Mrs. Dwyer says. "Really, it's hard to remember."

Matthew's face has an expression I've never seen before. Totally calm in a way that's the opposite of calm.

"I think we're done," says Matthew. "I'll walk Felicia to the train."

"Thanks," I say. "Thanks for the juice."

"You're welcome!" chirps Mrs. Dwyer. She pats my hand. "I hope you'll come by again!"

Matthew and I don't say anything at all till we're crossing Seventh Avenue, approaching the corner where I have to catch the subway back to Manhattan.

"Sorry 'bout that," he blurts suddenly. "Too much information, right?"

Too much? I don't think I've ever been part of a conversation where so LITTLE information was shared! But it seems like Matthew and his mom are both pretty good at keeping secrets.

"Maybe the data will be useful," I say, kind of embarrassed for him but wanting to put a positive spin on things. "Maybe we can form a hypothesis out of that 'forbidden fruit' idea—"

"Nope," Matthew says. "See ya tomorrow. Quarter to one, I'll meet you by the subway, at the southwest corner of Eighty-sixth and Lex."

"See ya," I say. And Matthew lopes off.

As I watch him go, I have a brand-new and unprecedented thought about Matthew, which is kind of amazing, when you consider the amount of Matthew-thinking I've done in my young life.

My thought is this: Matthew's not—you know. Perfect.

Even on a Saturday, crossing Lexington Avenue is a task that requires a person's full attention. With the grim determination of paratroopers leaping out of an Air Force jet into enemy terrain, Matthew and I step into the crosswalk, on our way to the Upper East Side brownstone of Miss Dervish Greenstream.

A yellow cab turns through the intersection way too fast, skidding through puddles six inches behind us.

Matthew shouts over the street noise, "Are you getting wet?"

I huddle closer under his umbrella. It's pouring rain and I'm lugging an overnight bag, because after our interview with Miss Greenstream I'm off to a weekend visit with my dad and Laura. I remembered to pack my pajamas, my toothbrush, my skin-care products, two outfits for Sunday, because who knows which one I'll be in the mood for, my notebook, my favorite pen, my other favorite pen, my French tapes, a choice of books (one trashy, one lit'rature), and some dog treats for Moose, their dog. The umbrella I forgot.

"I'm fine," I yell back. And who wouldn't be, sharing an umbrella with Matthew Maybe-he's-not-perfect-but-I-still-love-him Dwyer?

From the outside, 267 East Eighty-fourth Street looks much like all the other fancy brownstone houses on this posh New York City block. We climb the steep stone steps and stand in front of immense, black-painted double wooden doors, their panes of milky glass etched with interlocking, spiraling designs.

Matthew rings the bell. "Look," he says, touching his fingertip to the glass. "A double helix."

Before I can say anything in response, the great wooden doors open, and we get our first look at Miss Dervish Greenstream.

"Matthew! Felicia! Come in!" she says, like an old friend. "I've been expecting you."

After hanging our wet coats in the downstairs bathroom and leaving Matthew's soggy umbrella in an urn shaped like an elephant's foot (which Jacob later told us WAS an elephant's foot, how gross is that?), we follow Dervish upstairs.

The hall leading to the music room is dark, and the scent of sandalwood is everywhere. We sidestep past a dozen strange black suitcases, each in the unexpected shape of an exclamation point: long and narrow with a bulb on the end. The suitcases are well worn and well traveled, covered with baggage claim stickers and labeled FRAGILE in every conceivable language.

Inside, Jacob is sitting cross-legged on the floor, his sitar in his lap. One look at the long-necked instrument, its metal strings leading down to a small, round body made of an actual gourd, and I realize those exclamation-point suitcases must be sitar cases.

Jacob is chanting something that sounds sort of Morse code-y: "DA din-din da, DA din-din da, DA tin-tin ta, te-te tin-tin da . . ."

"Good, Shashti," says Dervish, pushing aside a gauzy curtain so we can enter. "A little faster now."

Jacob chants faster. The music room has beautiful French doors at one end and two enormous, multipaned windows at the other, overlooking a garden. The walls are painted a dark, glossy maroon and hung with tapestries, all embroidered with scenes from Hindu mythology.

Dervish sees me looking at the tapestries. "Those depict Tara," she explains. "The great mother, who reminds us to be still and look within."

I, of course, know all about this Goddess-Archetype-Within-That's-Inside-Me, but now does not seem the time to show off my grasp of the esoteric. Dervish smiles and gestures for us to sit. There are no chairs, but the floor is layered with patterned carpets and many large, lavishly embroidered pillows. The walls, the tapestries, the carpets, the pillows—everything is saturated with color and design. Vivid gold against dark purple, saffron orange, deep midnight blue, with bits of sparkling mirror woven into the fabrics.

Dervish folds herself neatly onto a pillow. In contrast to the kaleidoscopic surroundings, she wears a plain white T-shirt and a pair of baggy acid-wash jeans, which strike me as a bit 1980s, to tell the truth. Her gray-blond hair is cut in a neat bob, and she would not seem out of place shopping at Bloomingdale's. "Shashti tells me you are pilgrims, searching for enlightenment?" she asks.

"Shashti is my Indian name," explains Jacob.

"You search, but already you are wiser than many who call themselves teachers," says Dervish, "because you don't chase false images. You search for the truth. You search for love."

"We're, uh, doing a science fair project," says Matthew.

"Of course," she says. "And you love each other?"

Apparently, neither Matthew nor I know what to say to this, since we basically just stammer and go "Uh" while pulling at our damp socks.

"Of course," Dervish repeats, as if we've answered. "Such a strong connection. The past lives are many, many. And what can Dervish tell you about love that you don't already know?"

For a split second I wonder what it would be like if I started to refer to myself in the third person. Sorry,

Mom, Felicia has no intention of cleaning her room! What can Felicia tell you about dust bunnies that you don't already know? "We would like a specific example of two people falling in love," I say. "We want to know how it happens, so we can design experiments that will recreate the phenomenon under laboratory conditions."

Matthew looks at me admiringly. I realize I'm starting to sound like him. Does love do that to people?

Dervish nods and turns to Jacob. "Play for me, Shashti. Tales of love require music."

Jacob strums his sitar. It makes a pleasant, twangy sound, almost like a banjo, but as he begins to play it takes on a voice all its own, with sliding, complicated melodies in the high strings and a rhythmic droning underneath.

Dervish reaches for a small drum and starts to play along with Jacob—I mean Shashti. She strikes the drum with all the parts of her hand in turn, the palm, the fingers, the fingertips, each strike making a different sound. The drumming makes me want to clap along with the music, but I don't, since I don't want to miss a single syllable of what Dervish is going to say.

"I call my song 'The Tale of Tenzin and Dervish,' " says Dervish, speaking in time to the music.

"Hai!" Jacob cries out. It sounds like a little yelp.

"I call my song 'The Lovers on the Mountain,' " Dervish singsongs.

"Hai!" yelps Jacob. "Hai! Hai!"

Is he choking? I start a quick mental review of the Heimlich maneuver, but then I realize this is the sitar-player equivalent of shouting "Rock on!" to the singer.

"I call my song 'The True Language of Love,' " chants Dervish.

Matthew has closed his eyes. He's leaning back on a big purple-orange-golden pillow and looks relaxed and peaceful. I decide to close my eyes, too.

Jacob sways and plays. The chord underneath stays constant, but the music is continually changing nevertheless. And now, Dervish begins to sing her long-awaited Raga-Saga of Love.

Unfortunately for us, it's in Hindi.

And yet, while she sings and Jacob plays, a whole story unspools in my head, like a dream but clearer. It's about me and Matthew. We're climbing the side of a mountain. He slips, or maybe I'm the one who slips. Arms stretch out across a great chasm; we reach out to each other. . . .

Dervish has another student, so there isn't time to get a full line-by-line translation of her song, which was made up on the spot in any case and would be difficult to reconstruct. But the quick summary she gives as she shows us out of the house goes something like this:

Many years ago, she was trekking in the mountains of Nepal with a Sherpa guide named Tenzin. In a sudden storm, both of them lost their footing and nearly slid off the side of the mountain. Somehow they scrambled back onto the trail, but Tenzin had broken his left ankle and Dervish had broken her right big toe. By lashing their injured legs together, three-legged-race style, they were able to make it back to base camp, and there, on a slippery slope of the

Himalayas, they became passionate lovers until their bones healed and the lack of a common spoken language started to be somewhat of a drag, and anyway her return plane ticket from Kathmandu was about to expire and she was seriously jonesing for American comfort food like macaroni and cheese. So it was time to say farewell.

"When you've saved each other's lives, the karmic debt is powerful," Dervish says as we retrieve our wet coats and Matthew's umbrella. Matthew seems dazed. "It creates a strong, strong energy between you." She looks nostalgic. "Makes things pretty steamy, if you know what I mean!"

I wish I did know, but the only steam rising between me and my Darling Dazed Dawg is coming from a manhole cover on Lexington Avenue, streaming up in dirty gray puffs as we cross the street. The rain has slowed to a drizzle and everything is wet, wet, wet. Jacob has his sitar case wrapped in a plastic garment bag.

"See?" Jacob says as we duck under the awning of the King's Palace Hotel, on the east side of Lex. "I told you she was cool. She's an heiress or something. I think her grandfather invented Kleenex."

"You sound great when you play, Jacob," I say. "What was that 'dit dit da' thing you were saying?"

"That's just counting," he says. "Indian music has, like, a lot of beats."

"What kind of car does your father drive?" asks Matthew. He's craning his neck, looking down Lex. The King's Palace is where my dad is supposed to pick me up, but traffic looks gridlocked.

"A Camry," I say. "He'll be here. You guys don't have to wait."

"Nonsense! And leave a fair damsel in the rain?" says the noble Sir Jacob, shaking the drops out of his platinum dreads like a wet white poodle.

"Course we'll wait," says Matthew, leaning out into the drizzle. He's been strangely quiet since we left Dervish's house.

The doorman of the hotel has been standing behind us this whole time, in his red and black uniform and big bearskin hat, just like the famously silent and stony-faced guards at Buckingham Palace. But this is New York City, where everyone has something to say.

"What poifect gentlemen!" he growls, his New Yawk accent thick as the incense at Dervish's house. "You must be a special young lady to have two such gallant chevaliers!"

I want to point out to him that, technically, chevaliers would be on horseback, which neither Matthew nor Jacob are, but just then a white Camry with New Jersey plates pulls up in front of the hotel and honks. *Beeeeeeep! Beep beep!* That's my dad.

"Hey, sugar!" he calls out, rolling down his window. "Climb in, we're running late!" The trunk of the Camry pops open. I throw in my overnight bag and stretch high on tippy-toe to close the trunk. My dad gets out of the car to help, but Matthew is already beside me, easily slamming the trunk down.

"Dad, this is Matthew Dwyer. Matthew, this is my dad." This unlikely combination of words sounds fake even as I'm saying it.

"You're the one with the science project, right?" says

Dad, shaking Matthew's hand. "Super." Dad never used to say super till he met Laura. "The three of us are supposed to have a meeting or something?"

"An interview, yes," says Matthew. "When would be convenient?"

"Lunch next week? I'll check my calendar and we'll pick a day. Oh, you have school . . ." My dad's voice trails off.

"It's for a science project. It's fine, Dad. We're allowed to meet you for lunch, they won't mind." I'm starting to drip. "Can we talk about this later? When we're not, like, in a monsoon?"

"How do you do, sir? I'm Jacob!" Jacob calls loudly from under the awning. "Forgive my appalling lack of manners, but I have to protect my instrument!"

"Oh, howdy there," says Dad, confused by the presence of a second teenage boy when he thought there was only one. The thing about my dad is, he expects to be confused by my life, so he doesn't make that extra effort to understand stuff. He just focuses on what he does understand, like giving people rides. "No problem," he says. "Can I give you boys a lift anywhere?"

"No thanks," says Matthew. "I need to walk."

Much as I would love to have Matthew along for a ride in the Camry, I understand his point. I'd need to walk, too, if I'd just heard the Secret of Love revealed in a language I couldn't understand. Which, in fact, did just happen to me, and I wish I could say something to Matthew about it, but my dad is standing right here. "Looking forward to that lunch, sir," Matthew says, wiping the rain out of his eyes.

"Right, Tuesday, or maybe Wednesday's better—I'll

check my book and let Felicia know. Okay, let's hit the road, sugar, gotta go gotta go." My dad gives Matthew a hearty handshake, waves in the general direction of Jacob, and scurries back behind the wheel of the Camry. There's a solid thunk as he slams the car door.

Matthew looks at me. I feel a big drip of water running down the side of my nose.

"You're all wet!" he says.

"You too," I say. "Matthew—"

"Did you see anything?" he asks in a rush. "While Dervish was singing?"

"Yes," I say, surprised by his question. "I mean, sort of." It's true, I did have a vision, but is this really the time to tell Matthew about me and him on the mountain?

"I did, too. Like a movie in my head. Weird stuff I–I can't really remember," he says, his hair plastered to his forehead. "Isn't that dumb?"

"I'll see you Monday," I say, but what I mean is, don't worry, lots of people have visions, like Joan of Arc or Hildegard of Bingen, for example, and sometimes it means they're schizophrenic and other times it's just migraines but a few of them are probably channeling something important from the Great Beyond and by the way I am still CRAZY IN LOVE with you, Matthew Dwyer!

"See ya," he says.

And Matthew kisses me, quickly, right on my cold wet cheek.

As if on cue, it starts to pour again. I run to the passenger-side door of the Camry, waving at Jacob. "Bye, Jacob! Thanks!"

Matthew slams my door shut. I wave to him through

the rain-speckled car window. As my dad pulls out into the traffic on Lex, I could swear I see an actual twinkle in the eye of the King's Palace doorman, like a happy firefly in the rain. My dad honks his horn.

Beeeeeeeep! Beep Beep!

French Toast! For Breakfast!
Everything's Peachy in Lauraville!

My whole life since I was a wee little Kitten, every time I traveled over a bridge, whether by car or bus or riding a train, some well-intentioned grown-up would say in an excited voice, "Look! We're going over a bridge!" And I'd look. And in fact, it's always pretty interesting.

New York City has some of the coolest bridges ever in the annals of bridgedom. On the East Side there are those three famous sisters, the Williamsburg, Manhattan, and Brooklyn Bridges. They connect Manhattan to Brooklyn and vice versa, and they're so close together that no matter which one you're on, you can see that traffic is moving faster on the other two. Also in Brooklyn is the Verrazano Bridge, an astonishing piece of engineering marred only by the fact that once you get across it you're in Staten Island. More choices for crossing the East River are available farther north, in Queens, most notably the Fifty-ninth Street Bridge and the mazelike Triborough Bridge, which inexplicably manages to go three places at once.

But the crème de la plooz, as Jacob would say, the people's choice, is the George Washington Bridge, which is on the West Side of Manhattan and spans the Hudson River at 178th Street. For one thing, it's a beautiful sight, with its deeply curved suspension cables and open lattice-work of steel. It has a more glamorous setting than the East River bridges, with the elegant prewar apartment buildings of Washington Heights on one side and the lush green cliffs of the New Jersey Palisades on the other.

But the most crucial thing about the George Washington Bridge is this: it's the slender, twinkling leash that tethers New York City to America. We are just a little island out here, after all, a chunk of ancient rock sticking up from a deep harbor that just happens to be the center of the human-made universe.

That's why, whenever I'm off to one of my twice-a-month weekends in New Jersey, I always make a mental note of the moment when we get to the other side of the Gee Dubya, as we city folk call it. It's like when you're in a plane that's landing and you hold your breath, waiting to feel the bump of the wheels touching the ground. We are now arriving on the mainland. You are entering the Dad Zone, and thank you for flying Camry Express.

"Moose had fleas!" Dad says as he drives. The wipers give a lazy rhythmic thump every ten seconds or so. "We had to bomb the house. What a pain." *Thump.*

"You should use herbal flea collars. They're non-toxic," I say. *Thump. Thump.*

The wipers thump, Dad hmmphs, and we drive. Toll plaza, highway, strip malls, and multiplexes. Eventually we reach the exit that leads to Oakville, New Jersey, also known as Lauraville: The Town That Ate My Dad.

"We're getting pizza for dinner, okay?" Dad says, turning the wheel with one hand and rummaging for his cell phone with the other. "I'll call now and we can pick it up on the way home." This is another quirk of life on the mainland. You have to pick up your pizza. In the city, the pizza comes to you.

"Pizza's fine," I say. I close my eyes and let my head lean against the clammy, vibrating window. The nerve endings in the spot on my cheek where Matthew kissed me are still doing the macarena. Has a glimmer of X been spotted? I need to talk to the Kittens, quick!

Once at Chez LauraDad, we devour the bready, cheesy Jersey pie from pretty floral-rimmed plates at the big dining room table.

"Charles will be so excited to see you! He's getting very tall!" chitchats the ever-dieting Laura as she nibbles her way through half a slice. "Did your dad tell you they're reopening the pool club in June? How fun! I hope you'll come out lots and lots, that would be super! It must be awful spending summers in the city."

Charles is Laura's son, who's four and usually spends

weekends with HIS dad, the former Mr. Laura. But it seems they've summoned Charles back for Sunday so we can all be together, Brady Bunch style. Super.

"So that's the boy your mom told me about, huh?" Dad says, plopping another slice on my plate. "Seems pleasant."

Matthew? Pleasant? Brilliant, mysterious, lanky and witty and oh-so-lovable Matthew, pleasant? It's like saying the Taj Mahal is a cute little house.

"He's very nice," I say. "He's not my boyfriend," I add, to avoid any Mrs. Dwyer–like confusion.

"Better not be!" says Dad. He thinks this is funny.

"It's a science project," I say.

"Super," says Dad, through a mouthful of pie. "You still into the poetry? Or is science the new thing?"

Poor, poor Dad. I used to get really mad when he couldn't keep track of the simplest facts about my life. But then Mom told me the story about the empty boat. It's an old Buddhist story. A monk was fishing from a little boat in a river, and he looked up and saw another boat heading right toward him. He got very angry and started calling to the other boat to turn away, watch where you're going, stop, STOP! But it kept coming, and the monk got so furious he jumped up and down, yelling and hollering, till he almost fell out of his own boat. And then the other boat floated right up to him and he saw it was empty. It was just being carried along by the current. And the monk laughed and laughed.

After dinner, Dad and Laura tune the TV to something they think I'll like, and Moose climbs on the sofa and snuggles his big golden head in my lap. But I can't stop yawning, so nobody objects when I excuse myself and retire to the room Dad and Laura call Felicia's room, even though it has nothing to do with me. It's all princessey and decorated in pale pastel colors, like an Easter egg. It does, however, have a phone.

My first Kittencall is to Kat. Before I can even tell her about Dervish's house, the music, the visions, the KISS, she starts babbling at me. It is incredibly unlike Kat to babble. Something must be up.

"*Bleeping blintzky bleepskanya!* Felicia, you are reading my mind to call me! The grossest possible thing has happened! It's about Dmitri."

Who's Dmitri? I think, and then I remember: the creepy new accompanist! The gross old guy with the weird vibe.

"At the end of our rehearsal today he gave me a card," babbles Kat. "I didn't even open it till I got home, because I was too busy thinking about all the mistakes I made during rehearsal, and that the program I had picked was stupid and boring and maybe I should throw out all the pieces and choose different ones."

"You always say stuff like that before a recital," I say.

"Yes! And it's always true! But that's not the point!" cries Kat into the phone. "The point is, it's a love letter! Three pages in tiny little script . . .

" 'And so, my darling Katarina, I finally must bring myself to confess these feelings that are burning so hotly in my bosom. I watch you play for day after day and I dream I could be your violin! Embraced by you and made to sing with joy!

Yours, in every way,
Dmitri'*

"That's how it ends. I feel sick," says Kat.

" 'Hotly in my bosom' is pretty sickening," I agree.

"I don't mean the prose! It's just gross! He's like, thirty. And I can't stand that he's been watching me this whole time and thinking stuff like this without my knowing!"

We agree that Dmitri is gross, the letter is gross, and it's totally unfair that now she has to decide what to do about it because all she wants is to have a good recital. It's way too late to find a new accompanist, and despite his über-grossness Dmitri is an excellent pianist. And even if she could replace him, she'd have to make up some reason OR tell her dad about the letter.

"And that would be very bad," Katarina says in a low voice. "He'd be so mad. I don't want to think what might happen."

Poor Kat! I give her what assurances I can and tell her I'll see her at the Pound on Monday.

It's too late to call Jess now, so the tale of my kiss from Matthew will have to remain untold a little longer. As I slide under the smooth pastel-colored comforter, I tell it to myself once more, changing a few details as I go—move the kiss lipward, add mushy dialogue, tag on a happy ending and fade-out, in a little heart shape.

I also think about Kat's dilemma. The source of Dmitri's weird vibe has been revealed, and it is X. The dark side of X, the gross, unwanted X from an inappropriate person who has taken things way too far in his own mind.

I think this, and all of a sudden my cheeks flush hot and red like Jersey pizza sauce.

Is this what I'm doing with Matthew?
GROSS! GROSS! GROSS!

When I wake up after a night of strange, sandalwood-scented dreams, I resolve to monitor my own X more closely. The last thing I want is to be the gross[3] Dmitri of Matthew's world. That would be the biggest ewwwwww of all.

So many thoughts in my head! I know I'm supposed to be on poetry hiatus, but different rules apply in Lauraville, where I must use any means necessary to maintain my mental equilibritude. I grab my notebook and my second-favorite pen (because it's closer) and begin to work.

A Sonnet of X Gone Wrong

When X arrives, unwelcome as a flea,
Repel the itch with herbs and oil of tea tree.
Resolve to be a friend he's glad to see,
And not a total freak like weird Dmitri.

I'm trying to think of a better rhyme for "Dmitri" when there's a tap on the bedroom door.

"Oh, you're awake!" Laura says, waltzing right in. "Great! I wanted to catch you before you got dressed. Look, I bought you some clothes!"

Laura drops a heap of peachy-colored stuff on the foot of the bed. That's when she notices that I'm writing.

"Wouldn't you be more comfortable working at the desk?" she says. "It's so hard to get ink stains out of the sheets."

Felicia's Private Kitten Directive Number Iambic Pentameter: A Poem Cannot Be Written at a Desk.

"I'm fine here," I say. "Thanks for the clothes."

She brightens. "I was at the mall and they were having a fantastic sale. I thought this color would really flatter your complexion. I hope the girls' sizes fit!" Laura adds. "You're developing such a womanly figure!"

Furball alert: I gag on the word "developing." Gag.

"I'm gonna go tidy up before Hurricane Charles gets here!" she chirps. "And then we've got some superfun stuff planned! And French toast for breakfast! Okay?"

I'd prefer plain cereal, but okay! It's Sunday and this is what Dad and Laura do. Shop at the mall! And make big breakfasts! And plan outings! I picture all the exclamation points of Laura's speech as little sitars, swaying and twanging emphatically away. This strikes me as so hilarious I start to laugh out loud.

"Great!" says Laura, delighted by my obvious delight. "I'll make extra! With lots of syrup!"

By the time I get dressed and down to breakfast I'm fairly presentable, in my Pumas and dark hip-hugger jeans, with a black zippered hoodie layered over a peachy long-sleeved sweater. I push up the sleeves of the hoodie and make sure you can see the peachy sweater cuffs sticking out. This is a reasonable compromise, in my opinion.

If Laura is disappointed she doesn't show it. "See, Charles! I told you she was here!" she says. Hurricane Charles arrived while I was in the shower, apparently. He is actually crazy about me, which is fine.

"Feeeeeesha!" he yells, and runs to give me a big hug. We do our elaborate ritual of high fives.

"French toast, anyone?" says Dad.

"Ewwwwwww!" says Charles. "I want pancakes!"

"We're having French toast!" announces Laura, like this is a fresh tidbit of happy news.

"Hey, champ," says Dad, his voice sinking into a lower register. "It's good. You'll like it."

"Pancakes! French toast is too eggy!" says Charles, putting his arms straight down with his hands in little fists. I kind of see his point.

"But Feesha's having French toast! Right, Feesha? Aren't you having French toast?" Like, when did Laura start calling me Feesha? I have to end this, now.

"Chuck-o," I say. "You are a person of refined taste. I want to take you to the very best restaurant in all of New York. It's called the Moonbeam Diner. And everyone who works there is in a moon costume."

"Like astronauts?" he says, frowning but intrigued.

"Sort of. And when you get there, one of the moon people gives you a menu that's waaaay big, as big as you are. And inside is a list of every single kind of food there is."

"Pancakes?" says Chuck-o.

"Ten kinds of pancakes," I say. "And at the Moonbeam Diner you can have anything you want, because they have this big menu to choose from. But we're not there today. Today we're at your house."

"My house," he says. "No menu."

"No pancakes," I say.

"Just French toast," concludes Charles, scrunching up his face. "Can we play astronauts?"

"After we eat," I say. Laura puts two plates of French toast on the table in front of us. She's biting her lip. Dad is already eating and reading, in his own Sunday-paper world. And it's not even the *Times.*

After breakfast the day was spent mostly in the car, with stops at the petting zoo, the mall (there's always a reason to stop at the mall, it seems), the handmade ice cream place, and a McDonald's drive-through, after Charles went into meltdown and started screaming for a Happy Meal. After he got it he gave me the chicken nuggets, ate a few fries, and busied himself with the crappy toy du jour for exactly five minutes. Then he fell asleep in his car seat.

Dad drops off a sleeping Charles and a tired-but-still-"Wasn't that super?"-ing Laura at their house before driving me home. I give Charles a tiny kiss goodbye on his head, but he doesn't stir.

By the time the Camry makes it to the East Village it's after eight. It's cold and dark out, but the kind of cold and dark that's full of streetlights and yappy dogs being walked and boisterous people spilling out of cafes. Truly, there's no place like home.

"Bye, kiddo!" Dad says. "See you at lunch with what's-his-name. Wednesday or Thursday. I'll check my book and call you." We smooch and he waits till I'm safe inside the building before he drives away.

Upstairs, Mom's folding laundry and having her tot of Shiraz and grooving to some Bjork. That's a relief. Sometimes I catch her playing Billy Joel on the sly, usually when she's doing housework. Mom may run an esoteric bookstore in the East Village now, but once upon a time she was a nice girl from the Long Island suburbs. That's where she met my dad, in fact.

I know I'm supposed to wait to ask her about matters

pertaining to X until Matthew is here, because that's what Matthew and I agreed, but I was mulling something over in the car and out of my mouth it pops. "Mom," I say. "Why don't you get a boyfriend?"

From the look on her face, you'd think I suggested she join the NRA. She rolls an entire sock ball before answering.

"Felicia," she finally says, in a voice that makes her seem taller than she is, "relationships take *time*. Relationships are *work*. I don't *have* any time, and I have *more* than enough work, and I *was* in a relationship for many years and it's just not that easy. A *boyfriend*," she continues, and now she's looking at me sternly, as if it's me we're talking about and not her, "is NOT the only golden road to happiness."

But it couldn't hurt, is what I'm thinking. "I'm just saying," I say. "Dad has moved on. You guys just didn't have IT, you know? The X-factor. The catnip of Love. But maybe it's out there, somewhere."

Mom clams up, rather uncharacteristically, I should point out. She rolls another sock ball, except the socks don't match and she doesn't notice.

"Well," she finally says, with a rough sniff. "Even Meg Ryan got divorced, in real life. So who knows anything?"

8

Our Next Interview Leads to a
Barefoot, Bruising Lesson of Love

Randall's karate school (which he calls a dojo) is in Chinatown, and as we rumble our way downtown on the N train, zooming through subterranean tunnels that were blasted through the rock of Manhattan a hundred years ago, Matthew and I wonder what Randall's sensei will be like. I'm imagining a wizened Asian fellow prone to pithy, inscrutable statements. Matthew is picturing more of an action-hero type, sort of Jackie Chan meets Keanu Reeves. Clearly, there has been too much Blockbuster in our young lives.

We duck and dodge our way through the throngs of tourists and bargain hunters on Canal Street and arrive at a weather-beaten wooden door painted bright red, sandwiched between an herbalist's shop and an Off-Track Betting storefront. There's no sign and no buzzer, but it's the address Randall gave us. The door is un-locked. I guess if your hands are lethal weapons you don't worry so much about locking the door.

We push the red door open and step inside. Nothing but a rickety wooden staircase up a dark stairwell.

Matthew turns to me. "Creepy!" he whispers. "This is fun!" He's half right, in my opinion. But up the stairs we go, Matthew in front, till at the top we turn left and enter (insert sound of Chinese gong, rever-beverbeverberating!): the Fiery Dragon School of Self-Defense.

Yes, we're in the right place, except there's no Randall, and, as far as we can tell, there's no sensei, ei-ther. The only person here is a middle-aged man in baggy jeans, a black leather jacket, and a bunch of gold necklaces, talking fast in Spanish on his cell phone and drinking a Coke. He's leaning back in a black office chair, with his feet up on a rickety metal desk. The phone on the desk is ringing, but he ignores it and con-tinues talking into his cell.

Threadbare would be a kind way to describe this place, with its old brown carpet and walls in dire need of a paint job. Other than the chair and the metal desk, the room is empty except for a long wooden bench and a soda machine. The dojo itself is on the other side of a Plexiglas wall, with an entrance at either end. Like the curious Kitten I am, I take a step inside.

"Hey, *niña*!" yells the man. "No shoe in the dojo!"

"Sorry!" I cry, hopping back. Me and my shoes. It's so hard to get it right.

"Can we look around?" Matthew asks. "We're waiting for Randall."

"Ah, Randall!" he exclaims. We've said the magic word. "Okay, look around. No shoe," he says. He goes back to his phone call.

Barefoot, we enter. The dojo is basically an empty room with mirrors at one end, like a dance studio except the floor is covered with thick mats. There's a punching bag in the corner and a collection of padded clubs, very Fred Flintstone, hanging on nails along the far wall. Where is this sensei person? And where is Randall? I haven't really talked to him since Trip's horrifying pronouncement regarding the Randall-Loves-Me thing. Not avoiding him on purpose, mind you, just, you know, failing to acknowledge his presence.

But now Randall is late! Is he home changing his outfit a million times, in anticipation of seeing ME? Do Dawgs even do stuff like that? How awful, if so. I resolve to be more relaxed about my wardrobe selection process in the future, even if I know I might be seeing Matthew. I mean, unless it's CERTAIN that I WILL be seeing Matthew, in which case the wardrobe selection does deserve careful and prolonged consideration. . . .

This fascinating train of thought is derailed at exactly that moment by the sound of Randall speaking in a deep, abrupt voice:

"Osu! Onegaishimasu, Sensei!"

Matthew and I look out through the windowed wall of the dojo to the reception area, where we see Randall bowing deeply to his sensei.

And Sensei, now finished with his phone call and his Coke, is bowing right back.

"Hey, guys," says Randall, spotting us. "Sorry I'm late! I was calling to tell you but no one picked up the phone. I guess you've met Sensei Reynaldo."

"Not exactly. I'm Matthew," says Matthew.

"I'm Felicia," I say. "Sorry we didn't realize who you were."

"You think I be Chinese or something?" Sensei asks, smiling.

"Uh, yeah," I say.

"Why?" asks Sensei, with an even bigger smile. "Karate is Japanese. Me, Sensei, is Dominican. I make dojo in Chinatown because rent is cheap. And because I love dim sum!"

He bows to us both. We bow back.

"Felicia-Felicia!" he says, smiling. "I like you name. In Spanish means happy! You be happy always with that name, yes?" Sensei Reynaldo's teeth are very white and there's something sweet about him, now that he's being friendly. He looks at me and Matthew. "Randall say you have question for Sensei? You want to train?"

"We want to learn about love," I say, watching Randall out of the corner of my eye. Did his cheeks redden?

Sensei grins again. "Ah! We train karate, you train love! Ha, ha, ha! Wonderful. Come inside dojo. I teach love and karate, together! No shoe, please."

And thus begins our barefoot lesson of love from Sensei Reynaldo.

"Love!" says Sensei as we all sit down on the mats inside the dojo. "Love is why I start to do karate! Back home, in DR, where I grew up–"

"The Dominican Republic," Randall explains.

"Yes. Santo Domingo," says Sensei. "When I was little boy, same age like Randall"—Randall rolls his eyes at this—"there was a girl. Not so beautiful girl, normal girl, but most beautiful girl to me, you understand?"

We nod and he continues. "I love this girl, but she no love me! I try to win her, her—sorry, my English! What this?" He puts his hand on his chest.

"Her heart," says Randall.

"Her heart," Sensei repeats, working hard to get out the two *h*'s. He laughs. "I teach Randall karate, he teach me English! See? Everybody teacher, everybody student! In karate is same. Yellow belt teach white belt, orange belt teach yellow. Even most high-high-high black belt, always learn."

Randall nods at his sensei's words. He looks comfortable, for once.

"I brought her presents, flowers, I cook her favorite food and leave by her house. You cook?" Sensei asks Matthew.

"Not really," Matthew says, flustered at the question.

"Man should cook! No woman resist man who cooks!" Interesting idea. I don't remember my dad ever making anything but mashed potatoes when he lived with us. Now he grills. Now he has a deck with a gas-fired barbecue and silver-plated skewers from Williams-Sonoma.

"But my presents no good!" Sensei continues. "She nice girl, no mean to me, but no love me, you know? I cry inside, cry-cry-cry, but still, I love."

I feel my cheeks start to flush. Does Matthew understand that this is how I feel about HIM? And ohmigod, is this how Randall feels about ME? Randall's never given me a present, though.

"Then," Sensei goes on, "terrible thing happen! Her

brother have big, stupid fight with my brother, because of nothing, a car they both want to buy. Her brother say to girl, no more! No more see me, no more take my presents. How you say, Randall, no more?"

"Forbidden," says Randall.

"Forbidden! Forbidden to know me. Like I dead."

"That's . . . tragic," says Matthew, looking somber.

"Like Romeo and Juliet," muses Randall. I mentally award one point for literary reference to the Randinator.

Sensei beams. "It was miracle!" he says. "I bless that rotten car. A Chevrolet! Once brother say 'forbidden!' to the girl, she change! She say, I no let brother tell me what to do! She decide she love me now. She sneak out of house to see me, she tell me she want to marry! 'Take me away,' she say. 'Take me to New York!' "

And did he? Now we're dying to know.

"Well," says Sensei, relishing the tale, "the brother find out she love me. He come with his friends to beat me up. I always fast, so fast I could run from them. Most of the time I get away! But I hate that I scared. Hate that I run. That's when I start to train karate. Now I run for bus, and nothing else! I no scared. Randall, you scared?"

"Uh, sometimes," says Randall sheepishly.

"You champion. No be scared." Sensei sits back, satisfied. His tale is over when his karate training begins, happy ending and fade out. But of course, what we X-investigators really want to know is what happened with the girl.

"The girl! Ah, no-no, that's another story," says Sensei, waving away our question. We plead. "Okay." He relents. "Her brother get mad at someone else and she fall in love with him! I think she hate brother more than she love me. Later I join the army, I leave Dominican Republic. She still in Santo Domingo, I guess, I don't know. Old and fat now, maybe! But if I see her, she still beautiful to me."

"Why did you leave Santo Domingo?" I ask, curious. I can't imagine leaving my hometown.

Sensei Reynaldo looks at me as if I should already know. "To come to New York!" he says. "That's why everybody leave where they are."

When you put it that way, he has a point. "Now you watch us train. You watch Randall," Sensei says to us. "Your friend is great champion."

While Randall and Sensei go off to change their clothes, Matthew and I share our thoughts. Both of us feel there's a usable hypothesis lurking inside Sensei's story.

"Cooking, I'm sure there's something in that," suggests Matthew.

"No!" I say, excited. "It's the Romeo/Juliet Thing!"

He looks puzzled. "What kind of experiment could we design to test that?"

"Easy!" I say. "What if we weren't allowed to speak to each other anymore? And we had to sneak around and do everything in secret?"

Matthew starts asking all kinds of scientist questions, like how could we record the results of the experiment if we couldn't talk to each other, and how valid would the data be anyway, since we'd only be pretending, even assuming we got our parents and the Kittens and Dawgs to play along with us–

But now Randall and Sensei are back, each dressed in a spotless white tunic and loose trousers that stop right above the ankle. They bow in the doorway as they enter the dojo.

"This called a *gi*," says Sensei. "Nice, huh?" I have to admit, Randall looks totally different in his white gi, with a dark brown belt tied low around his waist. It suits him. His upright posture is authoritative, not stiff and uptight the way I've thought of it before. And his quietness, so shy and goofy in the outside world, seems centered and serious here in the dojo.

"Before train, we warm up," says Sensei. I'm expecting jumping jacks and maybe some stretching, but instead, Sensei and Randall both kneel on the mats and touch their foreheads to the floor. Then they sit up, eyes closed, and breathe deeply for a full minute.

And then, with a barked word from Sensei that I don't understand, they spring into action. Punches so fast the hands blur, kicks to the front, the side, the back. Leaps that turn in midair and land on a dime. Sensei grabs one of the padded Fred Flintstone clubs and starts whacking away at Randall, who blocks every blow so quickly I can barely tell which hand he's using. Then, with a high kick that snaps out from his knee at impossible speed, Randall knocks the club out of Sensei's hand, spins around, and sweeps his leg under Sensei's. A second later, Sensei is flat on his back on the floor, and Randall throws a lethal-looking punch that stops in midair, a half-inch from Sensei's face.

"KEEEEEEEE-YAH!!!" Randall roars. He freezes and stays there for a long, long moment.

"Yame!" says Sensei, finally. Randall drops his position and holds a hand out to Sensei, who takes it and springs easily to his feet.

"Not bad. Watch you leg! Back foot straight, not turn out," Sensei says to Randall. "Not bad." He turns to us. "You want to try?"

Well, of course we do! And need I say that I am experiencing a whole new appreciation for Randall? He's barely sweating. He tightens his belt with a tug and looks at me, not shy at all, with a half-smile that says, Look, see, this is who I really am.

"Okay, I teach two things. Two different self-defense," says Sensei. He proceeds to demonstrate how to escape if someone grabs you from behind. It involves reaching back and digging your middle fingers into this soft spot behind the other person's ears. We all try it on each other and are amazed at how much it hurts, even when you don't press very hard.

"Next, more difficult. Randall, you attack. Felicia-Felicia, you defense. Don't move, first time just watch."

Randall and I face each other. He assumes a relaxed, alert posture and takes several deep breaths. "Don't move," he repeats softly, almost as an afterthought, just as he starts to kick.

But how can I not move? His foot is flying toward my head at the speed of light. Without meaning to I take a step sideways and start to throw up my hands.

It's no use, though. My Kittenpaws are no defense against the Randinator's Flying Foot of Fate.

"I said don't move!" cries Randall, too late.

X X X

When Sensei removes the ice pack from my eye, the first thing I see is Matthew's concerned face looming in front of me. Randall is right behind him.

"Oh my God," gasps Randall.

"Whoa!" says Matthew. "Nice shiner!"

I gather from this amusing banter that, for the first time in my life, I am sporting a black eye. I immediately picture myself as Petey the dog, the patch-eyed mutt from the old *Our Gang* films.

"Felicia-Felicia! You look like champion!" says Sensei, grinning. "Come back tomorrow, I want to show you to my students! See this girl? First time in dojo and she go home with trophy!"

"I'm so sorry, Felicia," says Randall. "What a jerk."

"It's not your fault," I say, my head throbbing. "I shouldn't have moved."

"See?" says Sensei, handing me a Coke from the machine. "She champion, too."

My mom is not always the most coddling-type mom, but she does have an admirable way of getting on with things. After a brief round of hysteria when she saw my face, she pulled herself together, went to the medicine cabinet, and came back with a tube of arnica ointment. She dabs it on the bruised skin, saying, "I'm enrolling you at the dojo. You can take self-defense classes with this kid Randall and next time it better be him who ends up with the shiner."

And that would have been the end of it, as far as she was concerned. Unfortunately, while I was out getting my face kicked by the boy who may secretly love me, my dad called and left a message that tomorrow was the only day he could do lunch, and that Matthew and I should meet him at one o'clock at La Trattoria Ristorante Something Italian blah blah blah, and to wear a dress please if I could since it was a fancy joint and ask what's-his-name-who's-not-my-boyfriend to bring a tie if by some miracle he owned one.

Without even discussing it, Mom and I both knew that nobody's life would be made better by me showing up at a five-star restaurant in a pretty dress with a black eye, trying to get Dad to talk about love while his gazillion-dollar clients dined at nearby tables, watching and wondering if he beat his kid.

In fact, I was in favor of not mentioning the eye thing at all. All we had to do was postpone any Felicia-Dad contact for a couple of weeks by claiming I had the chicken pox (I felt sure he would forget I'd already had it). But Motherdear, invoking the O word, would have none of this.

"Better to be open, honey. I'll talk to him," she said, resolutely dialing the phone.

After brief ex-spouse pleasantries, she got right to the point:

"Felicia is not going to have lunch with you tomorrow—no, she's not, because—"

Pause.

"No, Robert, it's not 'my doing.' She's fourteen years old, she can form her own opinions of what you do with your expense account, she doesn't need me to point out the materialism and hypocrisy—"

Was that necessary, Mom? Big pause. She inhales, as if to speak. Exhales. Another big pause.

"Robert—" she says, trying to get a word in. "Robert,

please! Would you please listen? She doesn't want to see you because she has a black eye and she thinks you'll freak out."

Pause.

"Yes, a black eye. She's fine, it was an accident–"

Pause.

"Well, he was there, but it wasn't him, it was this other boy–"

At this point, Mom's end of the conversation goes quiet. Too quiet, as they say in the Westerns.

She says little else, in fact, until they're ready to hang up. And then all she says is "I think you need to cool off, is what I think. Let's talk again tomorrow. Goodbye." She clicks off the phone, expressionless.

"What happened?" I ask, my face shiny with ointment. "What did he say?"

"Don't worry about it, honey," she says, suddenly very preoccupied with an invisible spot on the kitchen counter. "You can have lunch with your dad another time."

Mom offered to let me skip school the next day, but I really didn't want to make a drama over this black eye situation, which looked worse than it felt. And I didn't want Randall to feel more guilt-stricken than he did already. After seeing his display of precision ass-whupping with Sensei, I have no doubt that Randall was more than capable of NOT kicking me in the face had I given him half a chance.

I was expecting people to ask questions and make sympathetic noises when they saw me, and I had prepared myself by practicing several short, whimsical explanations for my appearance. Polo accident, fighting off an alien abduction, that sort of thing.

What I wasn't expecting is what really happened, when I arrived at school that morning and found Kat and Jess buh-REATHLESSLY waiting for me in front of the Pound.

It's an overcast day, but they're both wearing sunglasses.

"Oh my GOD!" Jess cries, grabbing me by the shoulders. "We just ran into Randall and he told us what happened, you poor thing! But Fee! You will never, EVER believe this."

Slowly, Jess tips down her sunglasses. So does Kat.

Jess has a black eye, too.

So does Kat.

9

The First Experiment
Is Unleashed!

"My dad found the letter," Kat begins, once we've finished screaming and gone inside the Pound, fixed our
morning beverages (black decaf coffee for me, plain tea
for Kat, and coffee with steamed milk, two shakes of cinnamon, one shake of cocoa for Jess), and sequestered
ourselves in the Red Room, ignoring the many, many in-
describable looks we received from various Free
Children along the way.

"What letter?" I say, confused, having recently suf-
fered a blow to the head.

"The letter from Dmitri!" Kat and Jess cry, in stereo-
phonic Black-Eyed Kittensound.

I am dumbstruck. I know Kat's dad is a melancholy man, not terribly happy with his life as a building super-intendent in Washington Heights, with a wife who re-fuses to leave her dying mother in Moscow and a dying mother-in-law who, since her diagnosis, has so far lived eleven years and shows no signs of expiring anytime soon. I also know (from many late-night, tell-all Kittentalks) that twice a year, once on his wedding an-niversary and once at Christmas, Mr. Arlovsky is likely to consume an entire bottle of excellent vodka by him-self and then sleep for two days straight. But the rest of the time he is a doting if stern father, and Katarina is his angel, his princess, his reason for living.

"After I read the card," Kat explains, "I was so flustered, I must have left it on the kitchen table with my books."

"I still can't believe your dad read your personal cor-respondence!" declares Jess. "I'm almost POSITIVE that is a violation of the United Nations Directive on the Rights of Children, and I plan to look it up as SOON as I get home!"

"It wasn't his fault," Kat says. "He was going through the mail and the card was lying there. Once he started to read it, obviously it was addressed to me, but by then it was too late."

"Was he angry?" I ask, rather stupidly, since the girl is sitting here with a black eye.

"Furious!" says Kat. "But not at me. At Dmitri! Papa is so protective, you know, he's told me so many awful things about the way things are in Russia, especially for women." She sighs. "He wanted me to be a great musi-cian, not some mail-order bride. That's why we left

Mama in Moscow and came here to New York to begin with."

Before continuing Kat gives her hair a little shake, as if to shake off the sadness of missing her mom. Sensei Reynaldo was right. People from everywhere do leave their hometowns to come to New York, and often for good reason. But they have to leave an awful lot behind.

"Anyway," Kat goes on, more softly, "he didn't even know I was home, because I was in my room studying. I heard noise from the kitchen and went in to see. He was in a rage, throwing things. A can of peas went flying through the air and *bam!* hit me right here." She taps her purple cheekbone. "Poor Papa! When he saw my face he was beside himself. I've never seen him so upset."

"Tell her about the recital!" urges Jess.

Kat's expression darkens. "He says I must have nothing whatsoever to do with Dmitri. He wants me to cancel my recital. Find a new accompanist, try again in six months, maybe a year."

"No! I'm so sorry, Kat!" I know how hard she's been working. "You must be really disappointed."

Kat hands me a piece of paper. "I can't cancel, Felicia. Look at this."

It's a letter, on beautiful engraved stationery that reads "Argosy Records" on top. I skim the contents:

Dear Miss Arlovsky,

Thank you for your invitation. Please know that my staff have been following your career with interest and I am rearranging my travel plans to be at your upcoming recital . . . one of the most promising young artists I've heard about in a long time . . . eager to see firsthand if the rumors are true . . .

Et sweatera.

"It's from Edgar Chorloff! The head of Argosy Records! I've been trying to get him to come to one of my recitals for two years!" says Kat.

"What if you told your dad about this Chorloff guy?" I suggest. "Wouldn't he change his mind?"

Kat rolls her eyes. "It might make it worse! He thinks I'm not ready. But he thinks I'm not ready to cross the street by myself, either." A strand of butter-colored hair has worked its way into Kat's mouth, and she chews it idly for a second before she realizes what she's doing and spits it out.

"The thing is, when my dad calms down he'll change his mind about the recital, I know he will," says Kat firmly. "But by then it'll be too late. If Dmitri and I don't keep practicing I won't be prepared. And this HAS to be the best recital of my life!"

A group of Free Children wander into the Red Room. They see us. Their mouths drop open in horror. They whisper to each other and back out of the room, looking rather smirky if you ask me. One black eye deserves sympathy. Three, apparently, are nothing but grist for the rumor mill.

And speaking of black eye number three—it doesn't take me long to guess the source of Jess's shiner. But I guess wrong.

"Nope! It wasn't D. J. Amberson this time," laughs

Jess. "Though she did give me a bad set of skinned knees last week. I knew she tripped me that time, but I just pretended it was an accident." She points to her eye. "THIS was from those girls at her school! The ones she was singing with. They jumped me in the bathroom and said, 'Deej doesn't need any new friends' or something like that. Then one of them punched me and they ran away."

"That's horrible!" I say. "Are you okay?"

"It was a little scary," concedes Jess, before perking up again. "But guess what? Now Deej wants to hang out with me, because she's so mad at these other girls for trying to chase me off!"

"But I thought she didn't like you?" I ask, confused.

"She doesn't!" crows Jess in triumph. "But they only hit me because they didn't want me hanging around Deej, so now she's pissed at them and INSISTS on being friends with me!"

Kat and Dmitri. Jess and Deej. I'm sensing a pattern here, but what is it? It's out of focus, a blurry vision stoked by incense and twangy world music. "The thing is," adds Jess in a low voice, "my parents want me to cancel the peer tutoring program now! I know they're worried. But I'm finally getting close to Deej! I can't let her down."

"Isn't it strange?" says Kat. "I thought Dmitri was gross until my dad said I couldn't see him, but now I have to find a way to meet with him behind my dad's back! And Deej ignored you until these other girls tried to keep you apart, and now she wants to be your friend! I don't understand it."

But I do. I see it clearly now. It's the Romeo/ Juliet Thing!

In the meantime, let us both ponder—love. No topic could be more suitable for exploration by poets. For to be a great poet, one must grow a vast heart, big enough to embrace all humanity, and even, ultimately, oneself!

Be well and be brave, love and be loved. Until I return, I remain,

 Your fond fellow poet,
 Frasconi

10

A Subterranean Lunch Is Followed by the Tale of Cheryl and Robert

The Pound is not nearly as cliquey and gossipy as most other schools I've heard about, but let's face it: three best friends who show up on the same day with three black eyes (though only one apiece!) is such a mind-boggling display of synchronized swimming by the Great Beyond that it's bound to start rumors. Here are some of the better ones:

We had a three-Kitten catfight over a Dawg (and MANY names are being proposed as possible candidates!).

We had a "rumble" with a "girl gang" from another school, and we lost. In version B of this rumor we won, the other girls were hospitalized, and we're going to have to appear in court, drop out of the Pound, go to jail, or all of the above.

Our self-inflicted wounds are a protest against violence against women, and we will be appearing on *60 Minutes* to discuss our ten-point plan for legislative, social, and economic remedies to this ongoing problem. (Jess seems to approve of this rumor, and I can't help wondering if she started it.)

My favorite is that it's performance art, the black eyes are stage makeup, and we're secretly shooting a documentary film about the whole experience. The film will premiere at the Sundance Film Festival in Utah, to which the entire school will be invited in lieu of the traditional winter ski trip.

In the end, though, none of the rumors matter, because we know the truth. We also know that unless we DO something, the following dire consequences will ensue:

Kat's recital will be Indefinitely Postponed and her chance with Argosy Records, kaput.

Jess's tutoring project will be history and she'll lose the tiny bit of ground she's gained with D. J. Amberson, for good.

And the Search for X, not to mention my LIFE, will be over! Just when things were starting to get interesting.

(It took exactly three days for a full-color Brearley brochure to arrive in the mail, with a little Post-it note shamelessly attached: "My alma mater! Smiley-face, L." I guess they don't teach you at Brearley that people who use Latin phrases and smiley faces together are "Non compos mentis, look it up! Duh-face, F.")

For these reasons and more (for, let us not forget,

sad-face F. is still pining away for my Stray Dawg Matthew, who was suitably wowed by my Observations and Descriptions of the Romeo/Juliet Thing but remains impervious to my poorly aimed X that can't seem to hit the broad side of a barn), the Sex Kittens are all feeling a bit glum, too glum even to go to the Moonbeam for lunch.

Instead, Kat, Jess, and I don our coats and eye-concealing sunglasses (I borrowed a pair of supersized 1980s shades from my mom, who never throws anything away despite our lack of closet space), get take-out sand-wiches and corn chips from the corner deli to bring back to the Pound, and march grimly downstairs to the prac-tice rooms to eat. Technically you're not supposed to have lunch down here, but we can't bear the thought of sitting in the Pound's big dining room with all the stares and whispers that would doubtless swirl around us.

Jacob happens to be downstairs practicing his sitar, and when he sees us wander by he asks, politely, if he can join us. Due to his offbeat good looks (the tan has faded but the dreads are still platinum) and the aura of showbiz charisma he inherits from his mom, Jacob is considered somewhat of a hottie at the Pound, and he's prominently featured in the Kittens-have-a-catfight-over-Dawgs subset of rumors. But Jacob is not the sort who cares what other people say. And he's packed his own lunch of gluten chunks and pickled veggies on brown rice, so a subterranean picnic it is.

Jacob is trying to cheer us up by letting us taste the gluten chunks and guess what they're made of (the cor-rect answer is gluten) when who but Trip should appear at the door of the practice room. He presses his face against the glass comically. "I've been looking for you crazy kids everywhere!" his muffled voice says through the closed door. "Open up! I wanna see these pretty pugilists for myself."

We Kittens are in no mood, but ever-polite Jacob is already wiping the gluten juice from his hands and opening the door. Trip enters, talking fast and loud as a stand-up comic. "So, is it true what everyone's saying? That you girls wandered into an S-and-M club in the Village by mistake?" He gets a good look at us and stops short. "Oh, man!" Trip howls. "If only I had my digital camera—check out the bruised babes! This teenage trio packs a knockout punch of sex appeal! I'm serious, girls, we could do an awesome Web site."

Jacob turns to me. "Who's the asshole?" he asks politely.

Trip finds this hysterical. "Right on, brother! Defend their honor. I'm totally out of line, as usual."

"This is Trip," I say, in a please-calm-down voice. We don't need any more black eyes just now.

"I'm that filthy rich drunkard you've heard so much about," offers Trip helpfully.

Jacob eyes Trip with suspicion. "Easier for a camel to boogie through the eye of a needle than for a rich man to get into heaven, dude," he says.

"So true, man, that's why I'm not even trying!" Trip laughs. This attitude seems to pass muster with Jacob, and he and Trip do a little peacemaking hip-hop handshake, banging fists and trading high fives.

Trip gags at the gluten, so we offer him corn chips

and he joins us on the scratchy synthetic carpet. Now that our blood sugar is rising, we Kittens feel more hopeful and decide to do some serious problem-solving. First on the agenda is how to get Kat's recital back on track.

"I need a room with a grand piano, and my dad not to know I'm rehearsing with Dmitri," she says.

"Easy," Jess says. "The big practice room here has a grand piano. You can rehearse at school during the day."

"But that means Dmitri has to come to the Pound," says Kat, with an ewwwwww sound in her voice.

"True," Jess says. "But wouldn't it be better to have him here? Where we can all keep an eye on him?"

"That's the other thing," moans Kat. "I have to tell Dmitri I'm not interested in him *romantically*"—at this she makes a face—"but not upset him so much that it makes him quit being my accompanist, but be firm enough so he doesn't take it as a maybe when I ask him to come to my school and rehearse AND not tell my dad!" Ewwwwww indeed.

"We could hire a hit man," suggests Trip.

"If he's dead he can't play, dude," says Jacob. "I pity the Russian. It takes character to bear a broken heart with dignity."

"I know what to do." The wheels are turning ever faster in my Kittenbrain. "You need a *boyfriend.*"

"What?" says Kat, appalled. "I don't WANT a boyfriend, that's the whole point. Why can't I just say that?"

"Because," I say, remembering something I read once in the Unbound Page, in the Women Who Love the Exact Same Wrong Man Over and Over Again Till It's Ridiculous section, "Dmitri already has a whole fantasy life about you. Saying no is not going to be enough. If you already have a boyfriend, then he has to accept that he can't have you, plus he won't take it so personally that you think he's gross."

"So I just tell him I have a boyfriend?" Kat asks hesitantly. "Are you sure that'll work?"

"No!" I declare, realizing that it won't. "That's why someone has to pretend to BE your boyfriend!"

"I'll do it!" volunteers Trip. "Except, does it have to be only pretend?"

Kat's eyes are starting to flash sparks. "No thanks, Trip," she says, with an edge. "One unwanted suitor is more than enough."

"That's cold, woman!" says Trip, still smiling but clearly wounded. "Okay, no more jokes, not that I was kidding. I'll shut up now." Poor guy, I think, though I'm proud of Kat for sticking up for herself. Being in a practice room is obviously helping her stay in Violin Kat mode, flashing eyes and all.

Wait—did someone say unwanted suitors? Brainstorm!

"Randall will do it," I announce.

"RANDALL?" says Jess, eyebrows practically curving into question marks.

"Why not me?" says Jacob. "Or Matthew? I'm sure either one of us would behave like a perfect gentleman," he adds, inclining his head respectfully toward Kat.

"Of course you would," I say, refusing to contemplate Matthew being Kat's fake boyfriend, even temporarily. "But Randall is the better choice."

Now Jess gets it. "Because if Dmitri gives Kat any trouble," she begins—

"Randall," I finish, "will whup his lovesick Russian ass."

No one can argue with this. But Kat is dubious that

Randall will agree. I touch my cheek, which is starting to get a green tinge at the edges of the bruise. "He owes me a big favor," I say. "I'm sure he'll do it."

Privately, what I'm thinking is this: if Randall feels about me even remotely the way I feel about Matthew, he's bound to do anything I ask. Does that include pretending to be the boyfriend of one of my best friends? There's one way to find out!

(This raises the question of whether I'm actually curious to know whether Randall DOES feel that way about me. A question we will skip for now. Because anyone who's ever taken a test knows, if you don't know the answer, skip it and come back to it latah!)

"But I don't like to have people watch me practice," protests Kat. "Except you, sometimes."

"Then Randall's your man," I say. "You won't even know he's there. I mean that in a nice way," I quickly add.

Kat looks wary. "Okay," she says. "But there's one more problem. Good accompanists are expensive, and I have to pay Dmitri. Now that my dad is out of the picture, I'll have to come up with the money myself." She doesn't need to elaborate. We all know Kat doesn't have cash to spare. Her violin lessons alone eat up half her dad's modest pay.

"If this Dmitri dude loves you, he'd do it for free, wouldn't he?" asks Jacob. "I mean, I would, for an excellent lady like yourself, were I the gentleman in question."

"But we can't EXPLOIT his feelings for Kat, that will only ENCOURAGE him!" argues Jess. "It's absolutely necessary that Dmitri be paid. Kat has to keep this STRICTLY business."

True to his word, Trip has stayed silent during this whole exchange. Now he speaks.

"Hey, peeps," he says quietly. "I know I'm the interloping asshole who crashed your party. But I'd like to help." He's careful not to look directly at Kat. "Paying the lovesick Russian is something I can do. Problem solved. Okay?"

We all stare at Trip.

"Don't you want to know how much?" asks Kat in a shaky voice.

"Nope," he laughs. "Sorry to sound like such a spoiled trust-fundaholic and all, but the fact is, it really, truly doesn't matter."

"That was so cool, what Trip did, don't you think?"

"Yup."

"He's sort of surprising when you get to know him, isn't he?"

"Yup."

I'm desperately trying to start a conversation with Matthew, who's grown even more inscrutable than usual in recent days. As we walk together, not even the Barnum and Bailey streets of the East Village seem able to draw him out of whatever inner world is absorbing his attention at present.

It's not that we haven't talked. In fact, after my action-packed lunch in the practice room with the Kittens and Jacob and Trip, I hung out with Matthew in the lab for the rest of the afternoon, yakking about the Romeo/Juliet Thing (with mostly me doing the yakking) and playing with the bunnies. We created two complicated and completely scientific grids enabling us to track the Kat/Dmitri and Jess/Deej situations (Jess and Deej being a Kitten-Kitten friendship and not a Kitten-Dawg romance, but Matthew was quick to agree with me that there seems to be a friendship version of X as well).

Matthew concurs that we should watch these X-periments carefully, without interfering, sharpened pencils and graph paper at the ready so as not to miss any data points.

On a more cunning and selfish note, I also told Matthew about my freaked-out dad and the Brearley threat. The boring classes, the hourly bells, the dorky school uniforms, and the absence of Dawgs! The looming danger (which I made sound more imminent than it in fact seems to be, my mom having expressed a deafeningly Open response to the Brearley letter bomb from "L.," which sent Dad back to his corner, for now) that I could be snatched away from the Pound forever!

I didn't say this last part to him, exactly, but I did keep the phenomenal X-generating power of the Romeo/Juliet Thing in mind as I waited for his reaction. Would the threat of my disappearance cause any surge whatsoever in the flow of X between Matthew and me?

"Wow," he'd replied sympathetically as he clicked his stopwatch on George the bunny's latest run through the bunny maze. "That would suck."

Huh. Clearly, the Romeo/Juliet Thing, though effective in many cases, is not whipping up any X in this particular Dawg-to-Kitten, Matthew-to-Felicia configuration.

And so, with renewed purpose (on my part, anyway), we continue our research. Lunch with my dad is obviously nixed until further notice, but Matthew and I still haven't officially interviewed my mom. And that's why we're ding-donging and wind-chiming our way through the door of the Unbound Page.

Unlike my dad, Mom retains an encyclopedic knowledge of every trivial detail I have ever let slip about my life beyond her eagle eye. Sometimes this can be trying.

"Matthew!" she says, giving him a hug. "We've met once before, it was at that bake sale at school when they were raising money for the roof repairs. How are the rabbits? Any progress in the long-term memory protocol?"

"Some," he says, bewildered. Can she see his underwear through his clothes? It's possible.

"I made some twig tea. It tastes bad but you have to drink it, it's incredibly cleansing."

Mom has these smushy beanbag chairs in the back of the store so people can hang out. I've often suggested to her that if she didn't make it so comfortable to read in the store, people might actually buy the books, but she pooh-poohs this. "I'm creating community" is her answer. Whatevah. As we sink into the squishy chairs with our foul-smelling drinks, Mom starts to laugh.

"Oh! Robert called again." She laughs some more, which could either be a good or a bad sign.

"Robert's my dad," I say to Matthew, not wanting him to think there was some Robert in my life, in the Dawg sense. "What did he say?"

Mom stretches her legs out straight and flexes her bare toes. "Luckily for you," she says, "getting into Brearley takes more than a phone call even from a Laura, I mean an alumna."

When Mom makes word mistakes like this it's always on purpose. I mentally applaud the subtlety of her witchiness.

"Does that mean everything's okay now?" I ask, desperately hoping for a yes. If the Romeo/Juliet Thing is not working its X-magic on Matthew, who needs the stress?

"This seems more serious than his annual anxiety attack about whether MFCS is going to get you into Harvard," says Mom with a sigh. "He is just very very tense. I wish he'd do yoga or something, it would make my life SO much easier!"

"Sometimes I can't imagine you two ever getting married, Mom," I say, wiggling my butt deeper into the beanbag chair. "You're so different!" Matthew looks alarmed at my bluntness, but my mom and I always talk this way to each other.

Mom slurps her vile brew. "Yummy," she says. "I guess that's what you two came here to find out, isn't it? How Robert and I fell in love. Where the 'X' came from, right?"

We nod.

"And where it went," she says, more thoughtful than sad.

And so, she proceeds to tell us the story. Cheryl and Robert! A romantic tale of two suburban high-school kids. One, a rebel from the wrong side of the tracks; the other, a straight-A student from the original *Leave It to Beaver,* all-American family. One craves adventure, risk, and foreign lands, while the other longs for home, family, and a steady career.

What never ceases to amaze about the story of my parents is that Cheryl (who later became my wild, wacky mom!) was the straight-A, home-loving, nice girl from the sweet suburban clan. It was my dad—corporation-working, Camry-driving, Lauraville-living Dad—who was the bad-boy rebel, at least back in those distant Long Island days.

"We were crazy in love," remembers Mom. "Everything about him was dangerous and exciting to me, and everything about me made him feel safe and secure, like he had a home to come home to. We were the high-school sweethearts everybody knew would end up together forever."

"What happened?" asks Matthew. The story is so absorbing, we're both chugging back this awful tea without realizing it.

"I'm sure Robert would tell it differently," Mom says to Matthew with a smile. "But in my version, we grew up. We found out we were more than just the opposite of each other. Without those clear roles to play—me the steady rock, him the wild child—there wasn't much relationship left. By the time we figured all this out we had Felicia, of course. So it was hard to admit the marriage was over."

"I bet," says Matthew.

"It was the right choice," says Mom, with conviction. "We're both much happier now." This last bit is somewhat aimed at me, I know. Mom remembers, though I barely do, that I used to ask them both every day when they were moving back in together. I was little when I did that, no bigger than Charles.

"The funny thing is, we really haven't changed," says Mom. "Look at Robert! He loves the excitement of that crazy job of his, the fast pace, the big money, all the travel."

"But what about YOU?" I ask. I've never heard this part before, about how she and Dad haven't really changed. "Aren't you the wild one now? My groovy-hippie mom?"

"Oh, not at the core," she laughs. "I'm very practical. I run my own business. I serve tea, for heaven's sake! Having the store makes this neighborhood like a small town to me, with friends dropping in all day, talking about books." She stretches out one leg again and rubs her warm foot against my cold one. "And of course, being your mother has always, always been the most important thing to me." Awwwww. She likes to say stuff like that, it's sweet and yucky at the same time.

Matthew, I notice, is staring at us over the top of his tea mug like he's never seen two people carry on a conversation before.

"So you see," Mom concludes, curling her legs underneath her, "your father and I both got exactly what we wanted. But now we have to think of something to help calm Robert down."

"Paxil?" I say, not entirely kidding.

Mom sneers. "Aren't you cute?" she says.

"My eye's getting better," I say. "Won't he just forget about it eventually?"

"Honey," she says, getting that I-know-what-I'm-talking-about tone in her voice. "The eye thing was just an excuse. What's really bothering him is everything else: what were you doing in Chinatown in the middle of the school day? Why weren't you being 'supervised'? Why are you hanging out with boys who kick you in the face, accidentally or not?"

"Hmmph," I say, sounding just like my dad. I know she's right. That's the way he thinks, he just never says anything till it all comes out in an explosion.

"Remember, Robert was the wild one," she says. "He knows how much trouble a kid can get into."

"But, but but–" I say.

"I KNOW you're not like that! I'm just saying why I think he's overreacting."

"It's like he doesn't even know me." I admit that sounds very sulky-teen, but I feel entitled.

"I think it would help," Mom says gently, "if he could see some evidence of discipline. Structure. Academic rigor."

"Like rigor mortis?" I pun, meanly.

She rolls her eyes at me, like she wasn't the one who taught me how to make bad puns.

"What if we win the science fair?" Matthew suggests. I see he's finished his tea. "NASA and MIT and Microsoft always send scouts. That might impress him."

"Winning would be good," my mom says doubtfully. "But to be honest, I'm not sure the Secret of Love is something NASA is going to care much about."

"Respectfully, I disagree," says Matthew, sitting up as straight as one can in a beanbag. "In the short time we've been conducting this research, I've become very impressed at the complexity of the topic. Our Romeo/Juliet experiment is generating data we never could have anticipated. And now, based on your comments," he added,

"I think we may be ready to begin documenting Experiment Number Two."

I look at him, bewildered. What is he talking about?

" 'Do Opposites Attract?' " he announces proudly.

Way to go, Matthew! Just when you think he's lost interest, he comes up with something like that. Truly, a Dawg of Mystery.

"Interesting," my mom says. "Do opposites attract? I think, sometimes, they do. For a while, at least."

I give Matthew a quick tour of the Unbound Page before we leave, but I'm too embarrassed to show him the Deck of Hollywood Stars–what would a scientific DataDawg like him think of my tarot addiction? Little does he know how the entire Search for X emanated esoterically from this ragtag collection of showbiz personalities!

But while Matthew is in the restroom being cleansed by the twig tea, I scurry over to the deck to draw a single card, hoping for a quick read of our current situation. By now I know better than to ask if Matthew will ever lovemelovemeloveme. The Great Beyond does not play that game. Instead: Insight, I plead. Just give me some insight into this Felicia-Loves-Matthew thing.

You'll never believe what I draw.

Sonny and frikkin Cher.

Do opposites attract?

I got YOU, babe!

That night, tucked in my bed, I resist the urge to write a poem about this "opposites attract" idea. Instead, I make a list of the ways Matthew and I are most opposite.

HEIGHT
Matthew is tall (like Cher). I am short (like Sonny).
CONVERSATIONAL HABITS
Matthew listens and is quiet and full of secrets. I tend to blab everything, yak yak yak.
OUTLOOK ON LIFE
Matthew's worldview is based on factual data. I am fueled by vision, poetry, and inspiration (and DONUTS ha ha)

I stop here, flummoxed. These are certainly differences, but are they opposites? What if I took them to the extreme? Wore flat shoes to emphasize my lack of altitude, spouted confessional poetry nonstop, started reading palms in the Red Room? Would it turn the tide of X in my direction? It's a long shot, but I resolve to at least try the flat shoes. I usually wear boots with a chunky little heel, but tomorrow I will dig out the old Mary Janes.

I read my list one more time. The most opposite thing about Matthew and me, I can barely bring myself to admit, is that I am KOO-KOO-IN-LOVE with him—but him, with me, not. I wish I could think of a way for this most different of our differences to further my cause. Right now, I can't.

I turn out the light.

Maybe the shoes will help.

11

The Second Experiment Falls Flat, As the Crème de la Plooz of Footwear Proves That Opposites Only Sometimes Attract

The thing about Mary Janes is once you put them on, the rest of your outfit looks weird, and before you know it your three favorite pairs of jeans are in a pile on the floor and you're wearing a dark skirt and a peach-colored sweater and tying your hair back with a ribbon. By the time I'm done getting dressed—egads! I'm dressed for Brearley!

I fully expect my mom to comment on this suspiciously un-Felicia-like outfit before I leave for school. It would be nice if I could sneak out without her seeing me. Maybe if I tippy-toe on the tips of my Mary Janes—

"You look very nice," Mom says as she adds a tablespoon of nutritional yeast to her carrot-zucchini juice and chugs it down. (If not for chocolate-flavored soy milk, I would never open our refrigerator.)

I look very nice. Okay, I can deal with that. It's good to know I can pull off such a dorky ensemble, should I end up at Brearley after all. In fact, by the time I arrive at the Pound, I am feeling not so dorky. Maybe it's because the tattooed skinhead guy with the ferret who I see every morning on the M15 bus actually offered me his seat today. He's never done that before.

So why today? Do flat shoes give a Kitten some strange power over Dawgs? If so, this renders bogus a hefty percentage of shoe advertising, which trumpets the unwearably sky-high heel as the crème de la plooz of Sex Kitten footwear.

But, as Matthew might say, a true scientist must Observe and Describe the phenomena she actually, truly sees. She shouldn't put blinders on, stubbornly searching only for what she expects, or even wishes, to see.

No matter how hard she might be wishing.

"You look so little!" says Matthew, who's on all fours with his head in a fireplace. "Did you shrink?"

After a thorough search of the Pound, I've found Matthew in the fourth-floor study. It's freezing in here, and at the request of Ms. Blank next door in the math room, Matthew is trying to start a fire. But he cranes his head around long enough to notice that I've shrunk.

"It's the shoes," I say. He still doesn't get it. "They're flat."

"Huh," he says. "Aren't all shoes flat?"

Matthew Dwyer, sometimes I could strangle you. But before I can apply mental Wite-Out to that alarming thought, Jess pops in the door, chattering away with what can only be described as sitar-studded enthusiasm.

"You'll NEVER guess what I did! OH! Fee, LOOK how cute you are today!" exclaims Jess. "You should wear skirts more often. You have SUCH gorgeous legs!"

Yes, Jessica Kornbluth is the kind of excellent Kittenpal who always makes a point of saying the right thing in front of the right Dawg. One of many reasons we adore her.

"You need more kindling," she says to Matthew, ever helpful. "I'll go get some. But first! GUESS who's coming to the Pound tomorrow?"

Mr. Frasconi's not due back till Monday. The Easter bunny? No, Easter's not for weeks yet. My mind is still reeling from the utter, pathetic failure of the Mary Janes (one might say they fell flat, if one had the heart left to make puns), so right now I'm not putting two and two together that quickly.

"Who?" says Matthew, giving up on the fire and turning around, his face streaked with ash.

"Doris Jean AMBERSON, that's who!" says Jess. "After talking it out with my parents, it was clear they just didn't want me hanging out at Deej's school after I got punched there! But there's no reason not to continue our tutoring program HERE! At the Pound!"

"How did you convince her to come?" I say, standing up extra straight to compensate for my shrunkenness.

"I asked her!" says Jess, grinning. "And she said she'd ask her parents, and THEY said she should try it so she could 'come down off her stubborn high horse and see for herself what a different school was like.' They're not too happy about those tough friends of hers, either," says Jess. "I can't wait for you to meet her!"

"Perhaps she'd be interested in seeing the rabbits?" suggests Matthew hospitably.

"OH!" cries Jess. "Matthew! That would be AMAZING! Thanks so much, I bet she'd love it." Jess beams at me, her world in perfect tidy order. "I'll go get the kindling," she says, all but dancing out of the room.

I'm glad Jess is so happy, but it's only in-my-head glad. My heart is still flattened flat as a Mary Jane under the weight of this footwear fiasco. I know the feeling will pass, as feelings almost always do, but until then—

"Jess is very—impressive," says Matthew, oh-so-casual. "She has a logical approach to things."

"Yup," I say. Maybe I can borrow a pair of real shoes from someone?

"What color would you say her hair was?" I hear a Matthew-like voice saying. "It's not really red, but it's not really brown, either."

"Dunno," I mumble. Even gym sneakers would be better than Nightmare on Mary Jane Street. But Kat's feet are too big, and Jess's too small.

"I'm always fascinated by people who are so POSITIVE and OPTIMISTIC," Matthew says, with uncharacteristic emphaticness.

WHAT?

Okay. Matthew not being in love with me, I'm getting used to.

Matthew not being in love with anybody, I can totally handle.

But don't tell me Matthew likes Jess. That would be too much to bear.

"I wonder if she has any interest in science?" he muses. "She'd be an excellent researcher."

Something called REALITY crashes down around me, like the deafening ocean surf at Rockaway Beach, where I remember going years ago with my mom and Stuart, the only post-Dad boyfriend of hers I've ever actually met. Stuart, whom I never saw again after that torturous August day, with its hour-long subway rides to and from the beach and the bad hot dogs and burning sand and gallons of sunblock in between.

Of COURSE Matthew likes Jess! Jess is wonderful, energetic, a doer. She's extremely cute, in her Little Orphan Annie kind of way (I believe "auburn" is the word you're looking for, Matthew!). And she's logical. A realist. Incredibly smart. Just like Matthew.

I'll say that again:

JUST LIKE MATTHEW DWYER.

So much for opposites attracting! It seems my Mary Janes have worked EXACTLY the magic X-mojo I was hoping for, but with the usual tragic navigational flaw.

Yes, thanks to my footwear, the room has FILLED with X! And NONE of it is sticking to ME!

"I bet she'll really like the rabbits," says Matthew, turning back to the fireplace. It's not clear if he means Deej or Jess. "Don't you think so?"

"Of course she will," I say. My cheeks are so hot I could start that fire by sticking my face in it, kindling or no kindling. "Everybody likes rabbits."

✖ ✖ ✖

I am sitting at the counter of the Moonbeam Diner, alone, eating a slice of cherry pie with no enjoyment whatsoever. And the very, very, very last person I want to see right now is Randall.

"Hi!" says Randall, appearing out of nowhere. "I didn't know you came here. I love this place."

Before I can say anything that might persuade him to GO AWAY, he's on the stool next to me. "Wow!" he says. "You look so pretty!"

I start to conjure up a wisecrack about how surprised he sounds, but he babbles on. "I mean, you always look nice. But today you look extra nice. There's something about your hair that way. It's nice to be able to, uh, see your ears."

"Thanks," I say, fervently wishing one of us would disappear.

"Your eye looks better, too," he says. My ears, my eye. What's next, my glorious elbows?

"I'm wearing a lot of concealer," I say. "A *lot.*"

"Good," says Randall. "That's good." He seems encouraged that I haven't run away yet, even after that freakish barrage of body-part compliments. "Hey," he says in a different voice, "about that poem I wrote . . ."

"The seasonal reference was masterfully done," I say, sounding more bitter than sincere.

"Thanks. Anyway—when I wrote it, I was just trying to apologize. I didn't want you to think, like, you know . . ."

I think I do know what he's trying to say, but since he's hell-bent on having this conversation right now, when I am so not in the mood, I might as well make him work for it. "Think what?" I ask, all cruel innocence.

"That I was like, uh, hitting on you."

"But you already hit me!" I wisecrack. He's so teasable and I'm in such a bad temper, I can't help myself.

"I know!" says Randall, growing exasperated. "Listen, Felicia, I think you're a really nice girl and all. You're smart, and pretty, and, I mean, I like you a lot. But I know you like Matthew, and so I didn't want to be gross. I just think you're cool. You know?"

What's funny-sad, or more sad-funny, to be accurate, is how sitting here, hearing Randall profess his love for me, is so pathetically familiar. Even if I weren't in such a horrible mood, he'd seem sort of fumblingly sweet and even likable, but it wouldn't change how I feel.

Just like—but then my cheeks start to go cherry-pie red again, so I have to take a few calming breaths, since Randall's right here, mooning over me in the Moonbeam—

—just exactly like how the Search for X, though it might get me a first-place prize at the science fair, a job at NASA, and a full scholarship to Harvard, seems increasingly unlikely to change anything at all between me and Matthew.

Except, maybe, for the worse.

Poor me! Poor Randall! Poor unrequited lovers everywhere!

And then, my Kittenbrain desperate to think about anybody's unrequited-love woes but my own—

—and maybe, just maybe, wanting to console my flattened heart by finding out—purely for entertainment's sake, mind you—just How Much Randall Loves Me—

—I remember Kat and gross Dmitri, and that I need to ask Randall for a big, big favor.

"Randall, listen," I say, sweet as pie. "I need to ask you for a big, big favor."

"Sure," my willing X-slave replies, smiling and clueless, eager to be of service. "Anything you want."

12

I Try and Fail to Put the Kibosh on
Our Search and Encounter the
Walking Embodiment of X

Doris Jean Amberson is recoiling in horror from Frosty, who would really like to get a close-up sniff of her strawberry lip gloss.

"Do you mind?" she says, keeping her face as far away from Frosty as her long neck can stretch. "These are my church pants."

"C'mere, Frosty!" says Jess, retrieving the snuffling bunny from Deej's lap. "Frosty is a VERY unusual rabbit," she says, nuzzling her nose against his. "Isn't he, Matthew? Tell Deej about your research. It's INCREDIBLY fascinating!"

If she were anyone but her, it would be plain as the pink nose on Frosty's face that Jess was flirting shamelessly with Matthew. SuperKitten Jessica Kornbluth! My best pal and littermate, who keeps a picture of Gandhi taped in her locker! (Like, isn't he in a band?)

"The right combination of genetic engineering, pre- and postnatal nutritional supplementation, and intensive cognitive stimulation has resulted in some really impressive gains," Matthew explains as he scoops Frosty out of Jess's arms and noogies him on the head. "I'd say Frosty is about ten times as smart as the typical domestic rabbit. Smarter than a really smart dog, not quite as smart as, say, a four-year-old kid. Human kid, I mean."

Deej picks some silvery fur off her black turtleneck sweater with an expression of distaste. She looks around the lab, which is filled with puzzles and games and all kinds of special equipment for the rabbits to play on. "Maybe you should give your toys and your vitamins to a kid, then," she says, dry as a bone. "A human kid, even."

"That WOULD be interesting!" agrees Matthew.

"That's enough rabbits for now!" Jess interjects. She's eager to have Deej's first day-long visit to the Pound go well. Just yesterday, Jess cleverly and successfully argued before the MFCS faculty steering committee that students from other New York neighborhoods should qualify for the Pound's visiting student program, just as students from other countries do. If today is a success, Deej could be the first candidate.

"Thanks SO much, Matthew, the work you're doing is FANTASTIC!" says Jess. "We'll see you guys later. I want to take Deej for a walk in Gramercy Park before lunch!" She holds up her official, fully authorized key to the park. "Won't that be FUN?"

Deej waves a lukewarm goodbye, throws a baleful

look at poor Frosty, and follows Jess out. She seems a little tense, but who wouldn't be? The Pound is an unusual school, and when Jessica Kornbluth is your guide, you're going to have a BUSY day.

"That Jess sure has a LOT of energy!" says Matthew, starting to sound like someone I know. "That is SO great!"

I yawn. I can't help it. I was up really, really late, writing a whole batch of MatthewMatthewMatthew poems by flashlight (sorry, Mr. Frasconi, but you are NO help to me in Berlin and a heartbroken poet must do what she must!). This morning when I reread them, the poems seemed kind of angry. Which puzzled me, because how could it be Matthew's fault that he's not in love with me AT ALL and prefers Jess, the Energizer Kitten?

I yawn again, for spite. Matthew-who-loves-Jess is droning on about the Search for X. "Isn't it going WELL?" he enthuses, Jess-like. "I think this Opposites Attract idea is very promising, and I was wondering if you had any thoughts on that."

Of course I do, since by the way I was WEARING this experiment on my feet yesterday and I hope he and Jess will be very happy together and think of me now and then as I spend my pathetic X-less life alone. Maybe I'll get a cat when I'm old. Maybe I'll get twelve cats. Pets can love anyone, so they say.

"I've also been reviewing the rest of our interview data," he prattles on. "Another theme that seems worth exploring is the Mutual Rescue."

"Mutual Rescue," I say, in my crabbiest voice. "What's that?"

"Remember, from our meeting with Dervish Greenstream?" says Matthew, all chipper. "She said when you've saved each other's lives the karmic something-or-other is very powerful. I'm sure she was talking about X!"

What I know that Matthew doesn't, yet, is that I am SO OVER the Search for X. I'm serious. What's the point? I mean, I may not know WHAT X is, but I know exactly WHERE it is.

It's in Matthew, Jess, Kat, Trip, and Meg Ryan.

It used to be in Mom and Dad, but it's not anymore.

And it's definitely NOT in me.

But out of sheer habit, my brain tries to imagine how we would accomplish this Mutual Rescue experiment. I know! We could have Matthew and Jess jump out of an airplane together, with only one parachute between them. . . .

Alors! That's mean. And totally unfair to Jess, who is an innocent and unknowing participant in my secret jealous X-drama. Besides, she's never said anything to me about liking Matthew. But then again, how could she, when I've been so MatthewMatthewMatthew all year?

Breathe in, breathe out. Okay. If I take that logical approach to things that Matthew finds so X-citing in OTHER people, I must conclude that I don't have any way of knowing how Jess feels unless I ask her, which I plan to do as soon as possible. In the meantime, there's something else I must do. And that is put the kibosh on the Search for X.

"Matthew," I begin, sounding all singsongy like my mom, "what if our Search for X is just—a bad idea?" I venture this calmly, pleasantly. No need for drama. I want our research to die a painless, natural death. "Maybe you should present the rabbits at the science fair instead. They're INCREDIBLY fascinating, you're bound to win!"

Have I always been this evil? I smile at him, as if saying, See, problem solved, no hard feelings, don't-bother-getting-up-I'll-let-myself-out and *au revoir*!

Matthew smiles back at me, as if saying, Buck up, partner, Marie Curie had bad days, too! "The rabbits are for senior year," he says. "Did you know that I've been raising the IQ of each generation by an average of ten points? I can breed three generations of rabbits every term. By the time I graduate, Frosty will look like a dumb bunny compared to the rabbits I'll have then."

I know I said no drama, but for some reason this makes me furious. "Don't say that about Frosty!" I cry. "That's not fair!"

Matthew looks surprised. "Why not?" he asks. "Frosty's a real achievement, but I know I can do better."

But I've lost it, and I don't even know why, and words pour out of my mouth as if someone else is saying them. "So fine!" I yell. "What are you going to do with him, then? Sell him to a pet shop? Just get rid of him, like you don't care about him?"

Like you don't care about ME or ANYTHING but your stupid DATA and Jess-Jess-Jess-Jess-JESS?, my unbelievably mean, inner hurt-and-angry voice screams.

I have gone way, way, unforgivably too far, in my own mind. But Matthew, not knowing this, just looks at me with that calm expression I saw on his face when we were interviewing his mom.

"You could have him, if you want," he offers after a moment. "He really likes you."

"I'm sorry, Matthew," I stammer. "But I'm not sure I want to do this anymore."

"I know how you feel," Matthew says. He feeds Frosty a lettuce treat. "Science is hard."

"Fee! FIRST of all, I would NEVER go out with Matthew, knowing how you feel about him!"

Jess is looking at me so intently her face seems to be floating somewhere in front of her body.

"If you like him, you should, though," I say, sniffling. "I mean, he's never been interested in me anyway. Oh, Jess! I feel so stupid!" And that is the truth of it.

We're sitting on a bench inside Gram, near the center of the park. Deej is a little ways off, examining the statue of Edwin Booth. After my almost-outburst at Matthew, I knew I had to talk to Jess pronto, and I knew she was in Gram with Deej. I only had to run around the perimeter breathless and crying twice before I found them and got their attention so Jess could let me in through the gate.

"I would NEVER do that," Jess repeats, "because I think you would be really sad if I did, and you're my FRIEND!" She hugs me to prove her point. "Plus, I can honestly say I'm NOT interested in Matthew. I mean, he's perfectly nice," she adds, far too polite to disparage my taste in Dawgs.

"But why not?" I whine, stubborn as a stump, wiping my nose with the tissue Jess has magically provided. "I mean, I look at Matthew and I get all fluttery inside. I mean, I used to. Okay, I still do, but it's OVER! Totally, completely OVER! Even though it never really was!" Trying to put this into words is giving me a major headache.

"He's perfectly nice," Jess repeats gently. "He just doesn't do it for me." One might say Jess finds no single aspect of Matthew offputting in any way. "Maybe he's a little . . . distant or something. I like guys who are more affectionate."

"He's affectionate with the rabbits," I say, startled by the fact that she has a point.

"Of course he is. But I'm not a rabbit!" she says. "And neither are YOU." This seems to settle the matter for Jess. "So! What's going on with Randall?" she asks.

"Randall! Nothing!" I burble. "I mean, nothing. I mean, the other day he wrote me a poem. And then I ran into him at the Moonbeam and he told me I was smart and pretty and he liked me. But other than that . . ."

"WHAT? He wrote you a POEM? Ohmigod, that is so ROMANTIC!" Jess's dark, pupil-less eyes glitter with excitement. "What was it about?"

"About kicking me in the face," I say. "Listen, Jess, it's just like you said. Randall's perfectly fine, he just doesn't–I don't know! He's not my idea of what a boyfriend should be!"

"What do you feel when you see him?" she asks.

"It's not what I feel!" I say, temples throbbing. "It's what I DON'T feel! When I'm with Randall, I don't feel–"

"Anxious?"

"Yes. I, mean, no! I mean, he doesn't make me–"

"Insecure? Obsessed?"

"Jess!"

"Jealous?"

Jess's ability to sink a basket every time she shoots can be incredibly irritating when you're the hoop. I clam up. And anyway, Deej is coming back.

"To be, or not to be!" Deej calls out, laughing. "That statue gives me a chill. He looks like he's about to talk."

Jess, who knows all about her own tendency to be a know-it-all, now shows admirable self-control by saying only this, to me:

"Huh. I guess Randall's NOT for you, then."

Nevertheless, her point has been made. As Jess and Deej start chatting about Edwin Booth, *Hamlet,* the assassination of Abraham Lincoln, and other topics, I resolve to pay more careful attention to my feelings the next time I see Randall.

Perhaps I've been unfair. Perhaps there's more to Randall than meets the accidentally blackened eye.

The next time I see Randall, he is standing outside the big practice room in the basement of the Pound, affectionately smooching Katarina Arlovksy on the cheek.

"Bye, honey!" he says to her, loudly enough to be overheard. "Have a good rehearsal. I'll be back later. Call me if you need me!" He taps his belt as if he carries a cell phone there, which I know he doesn't. No cell phones in the Pound, it's one of the rare rules around here.

Kat puts her arms around Randall and gives him a hug. "Thanks, sweetie!" she says, in a voice that doesn't sound like her. "I'll see you later!"

"Bye, shnooky!"

"Bye, honey bun!"

Kat sees me and rolls her eyes.

A deafening Russian cacophony of pianistic suffering cascades out of the big practice room behind her.

She gestures for me to come closer, and she speaks pianissimo to me and Randall. "Dmitri didn't take it that well," she whispers, panicky. "We're supposed to be practicing the Haydn but all he'll play is Rachmaninoff! I want you to come back in *one* hour! Okay?"

"Okay, bye darling!" says Randall loudly. "Bye-bye, cutie pie!"

Randall gives her another peck. Pale and nervous, Kat retreats into the practice room.

"We have an hour," Randall says to me, quite pleased with his performance. "Wanna do lunch?"

A mysterious pang is forming somewhere inside me. Is it hunger? I take a moment to pay careful attention to my feelings, and what I'm feeling is this:

When I asked Randall-Who-Loves-Me to pretend to be Kat's boyfriend, I didn't think he'd be so *bleepsky-smooching-cutie-pie* GOOD at it.

"Sure," I say, beyond confused. "Let's eat."

Randall, who is taking his responsibility as Kat's protector quite seriously, does not want to leave the building, so we're stuck eating at the Pound. The food here is not your usual school cafeteria fare. It's more like what you'd find at an organic multi-ethnic gourmet restaurant, which is fine when you're in the multi-ethnic gourmet mood, but not on days like today, when a Kitten needs comfort and wants a grilled cheese sandwich.

I settle for two granola bars and some chocolate milk and follow Randall into the dining room. The Pound's rumor mill has definitely slowed down as the three black-eyed Kittens have healed, but I know that dining tête-à-tête with Randall will rev it up again. *Tant pis!* Or as we say in English, like I care at this point.

To tell the truth, I both dread and crave the chance to spend this hour with Randall, sifting through my feelings and looking for a trace of Felicia-and-Randall X. Luckily for my ambivalence, Jess and Deej—and, interestingly, Trip—are at a table in the corner. I can tell by the way Trip's sitting that he's been sending megawatts of flirty rich-boy charm in Deej's direction. It must be her five minutes.

Jess is, of course, superhappy to see me, and Randall, and especially me with Randall. "How's Kat?" she asks us. "What's happening with Dmitri?"

"He's playing Rachmaninoff, really loud," I say.

"Is that bad?"

"Kat seemed to think so."

As Jess starts to fill Deej in on the saga of Kat and Dmitri, her tale is interrupted by the ring of Trip's cell. Trip seems to have a special dispensation on the Pound's no-cell-phone rule, which the rest of us have chalked up to the Mysterious Privileges of the Rich. He always carries one but I've never seen him use it, until now.

"Hi, buddy, wassup?" he says quietly into the phone. "Sure. Yup. No worries, I'm clean as a whistle. You outside now? Be right there." He hangs up. "Be back in a sec, beloveds," he says to us. "I gotta go pee in a cup." And he leaves.

We're all confused. "What was that?" asks Randall, concerned. "Is he sick?"

Deej looks like she's about to say something, but busies herself with her food instead. Curried root vegetables with apricot chutney over basmati rice. It smells delicious. Kraft American singles on Wonder bread would also be good right about now.

When Trip returns, he sits down and resumes eating without comment.

"Everything okay?" asks Jess after a moment.

Trip smiles. "That was my friend calling. My P.O. He likes to check up on me."

Deej pushes away her plate and fixes Trip with a look.

"You're on parole?" she asks pointedly. "And what did you do? What did a rich boy like you need to steal?"

If I may speak for Randall and Jess as well as myself, I'd say we are as shocked by the blunt force of Deej's question as we are at learning that Trip is on parole. But Trip doesn't flinch.

"I'll tell you what I did," he says softly. "I fell in so deep with the wrongest crowd you can imagine, I almost screwed up my whole life trying to climb out."

"I did that, too," Deej says. Her voice is low and compassionate. "That's my old crew. The ones that picked on Jess."

"They weren't so bad," says Jess quickly.

"We were tighter than tight till this year," says Deej, sounding sad. "Now they're in high school, they think they're all grown, too cool for school, going too far with everything, telling me to do the same." She turns to Jess.

"That's why I didn't want them seeing me hang out with you. Sorry I tripped you that time! I figured if I did they'd leave you alone. They get mad when I get tight with other girls."

Jess taps her eye. "I noticed!" She laughs.

"You're lucky that's all you got!" says Deej. "They're still my friends," she adds after a moment. "But I don't wanna do what they do."

Trip's been taking in her story like he's having his fortune told. "Been there," he says softly. "Believe me, I have."

Are Trip and Deej opposites? Or the opposite of opposite? Before I can decide, Trip raises his glass of iced tea. "It's not champagne, but even the sober are allowed to pretend. To new friends!" he says warmly. "I'm glad to have met you, Deej."

"Yes!" says Jess. "We're all so glad to have you here. Even if it's just for today. But I hope it's not!"

"I'm glad, too," says Deej, sounding surprised. "Man, this place is sure not what I expected!"

Jess and Deej insist on going downstairs with Randall and me after lunch to check up on Kat and check out Dmitri, and Trip clearly would like to continue checking out Deej, so after lunch the five of us troop downstairs.

I'm feeling grateful for this Matthew-free midday adventure. It's distracting me from the broken heart that's lying in itty-bitty shards someplace inside me, near the liver, it feels like. There's no palpable X zinging between me and Randall, but it was not unpleasant to watch him eat, which I'm taking as a good sign.

The big practice room has Plexiglas windows along the top half of one wall. We don't want to be conspicuous, so the five of us crouch down on the carpet and sneak a peek above the bottom edge of the window.

"OhmiGOD!" chokes Jess. "LOOK at him!"

There's Dmitri, all right. He's at the piano. I blink hard, but it's not a vision.

"Lord!" breathes Deej, awestruck. "Have. Mercy."

It appears that gross-gross-gross, hotly-in-my-bosom Dmitri looks an awful lot like Johnny Depp. Dark hair, dark eyes, sculpted cheekbones, stern jaw but with soft, little-boy lips.

We can't stop staring. Trip and Randall are looking at us like we've gone insane. Jess's eyes are so dark you can't really see into them, but if they weren't I know they'd have little Xs floating in them right now.

It's hard to hear through the Plexiglas, but it appears that Kat and Dmitri are having an argument. He's gesturing wildly and talking fast, and she is standing with one hand on her hip, tapping her bow on the edge of the piano in a very impatient way.

Randall presses his ear to the glass. "Boeing, I think that's what he's saying," he reports.

"Boeing?" whispers Jess, alarmed. "A Boeing? That's a PLANE! Maybe he wants her to fly away with him! Maybe she's saying no and he won't listen! Maybe we should do something!"

"Bowing," I say. "It's a violin thing."

That's when Kat sees our $5 \times 2 = 10$ eyes peering through the window. Poor Kat! She hates to be watched, but she did ask us to check up on her. Randall stands up straight as an arrow and marches to the practice-room door. "How's it going, baby doll?" he booms.

"Fine," says Kat, who clearly has the situation well in hand. "Thanks, we're fine. I'll see you later, okay? End of day is fine."

That's when I notice Dmitri again, through the window—he's kind of hard NOT to notice, but I especially notice him right now because of the look on his face. He's watching Kat and Randall, and something changes. His Johnny Depp lips form the shape of an O. His cheeks start to flush, red as borscht.

"We have a lot of work to do," says Kat, shooing Randall out and closing the door. "Thanks! Bye!"

"She's fine," pronounces Randall. "Our work here is done!"

Poor Dmitri, I can't help thinking. Externally speaking, he is the Walking Embodiment of X, but even this is not enough to carry the day with Violin Kat, who simply has other things on her mind. No one's X is foolproof, apparently.

And, okay. I will admit this. Seeing Randall act all boyfriend-like to Kat is making him seem, I don't know . . . boyfriend-like?

"What are all these rooms for?" asks Deej, looking down the long hallway. There is a subtle hum in the air, the overheard strains of all the different kinds of music being played at once, muffled and mixed together.

"These are the practice rooms," says Trip with a grand gesture, like this is his house.

"All these rooms!" exclaims Deej, tiptoeing down the hall in wonder. "For practicing music? Really?"

She turns and looks at Jess, her face radiant. "Can I?"

Jess grins at Deej and opens the door of the nearest empty room.

"Do you play?" asks Randall, impressed.

"She SINGS," Jess declares. "Deej sings like an angel."

Trip stops short and leans against the wall as if he's about to melt. "Deej, honey, you are getting more dangerous by the minute," he says. "That's like, magic to me. I can't even carry a tune."

Deej skips into the practice room and closes the door. "Can you hear me from outside?" she shouts.

"No, not too much, tiny bit!" we call back, fibbing a little.

"Gimme a holler later, then! I'm gonna be a while!" Deej yells through the door.

And then Deej starts to sing.

Trip plops down on the floor, right where we're standing. "You all go about your day," he says to me and Jess and Randall. "I'm gonna stay here and listen to the music."

And he crosses his legs in the shape of an X, and leans back against the wall, and closes his eyes.

I could be wrong, but it looks he plans to stay for way more than five minutes.

Lucky

13

The Third Experiment Results in an X-Cellent Mutual Rescue!

"**A**re you mad at me?"

I can't believe Matthew is asking me this. It's been like, a week since the don't-you-care-about-Frosty incident. And I haven't been avoiding him, exactly. It's just that I don't want to search for X anymore, and I don't want to hear Matthew nattering about how great Jess is anymore, and so I've been keeping busy doing, you know, stuff. Lots of stuff to do. But I finally ran out of stuff, and it's the first time since the Frosty incident that I've agreed to go to the Moonbeam in the afternoon with Matthew, like we used to do almost every day.

I don't want to be here, but what choice do I have? There are only two more weeks till the science fair, and kiboshing the Search for X has proven impossible. Not only is Matthew not taking my bitter-quitter attitude seriously–Matthew Dwyer, miss the science fair? Unthinkable!–but there's the small matter of Fatherdear.

Dad and I spent my most recent excruciating weekend in Lauraville performing superhuman feats of not talking about my eye, or Brearley, or the out-of-control nature of my wastrel life. Instead, we passed the time being very very tense, watching TV, and wandering the mall (and for once I was grateful for Laura's endless spewing of chitchat, which significantly reduced the danger of actual communication).

But in the Mysterious Grown-up Realm, somewhat outside my Kittenradar, Cheryl-versus-Robert negotiations have been ongoing, with Discipline, Structure, and Academic Rigor Mortis the recurring buzzwords. I knew I was doomed the night Mom got off the phone with him and sounded all cheerful.

"I just talked to your dad," she announced, like I couldn't tell who it was, with all her Robert-pleases and Robert-listen-to-mes. "He says he's reserving judgment for now, but only because he is VERY impressed that you're doing a project for the science fair." She sounded quite pleased with herself. "So you better come up with something GREAT!"

Great. So now I have two weeks to discover the Secret of Love, which I already know doesn't apply to me anyway, and during which time I get to watch the Dawg I love be in love with someone else. Sounds fun, *n'est-ce pas?*

At least the Opposites Attract data is finally pouring

in. In fact, this X-periment is being played out in IMAX proportions in front of our very eyes, as Trip and Deej continue to toss the X back and forth like a Frisbee.

And Deej is now officially a visiting student! After she discovered the practice rooms and had some very fruitful conversations with the Pound's Master Music Mentors, she decided to give the Manhattan Free Children's School a chance, at least till the end of freshman year. Whether meeting Trip had anything to do with her decision I don't know, but Matthew and I are Observing their budding romance carefully and taking copious notes.

We still don't know what to do about a Mutual Rescue experiment, since everything we think of sounds life-threatening and I don't need a repeat of the black eye situation. Nor do I know what I want to eat, because this gargantuan menu at the Moonbeam offers way too many choices. But I do know how to answer Matthew's question.

"No!" I lie, brazen as Charles when he's elbow-deep in the cookie jar. "Of course I'm not mad at you. Why would I be mad at you?"

"I don't know." He shrugs. "About Frosty, maybe? Or about, you know. You and me. The X thing."

Oh, THAT old thing! "Listen, Matthew," I say, strictly business. "I know how you feel. You know how I feel. We're friends, right? We're partners in science."

He looks a little pained. "That's what I thought, too. But lately I've been thinking–no, I've been feeling–the thing is, Felicia–"

OhmiGOD! He's going to tell me about his CRUSH

on JESS! I pray for a waitress to interrupt, but all the Moonies in their gibbous moon T-shirts are waxing and waning elsewhere.

"The thing is, I really like, uh, Jess," Matthew says, staring deeply into the holes of a saltshaker. "I think I have for a while, but I didn't realize it, I guess. And then I had to write that essay, remember, when we traded homework assignments?"

—To tell the truth—

"And then I had this weird vision at Dervish's house, and Jess was in it—"

—although I understand these sensations intellectually I don't really have direct experience—

"—and, anyway," Matthew says, more softly, "until you and I started talking so much about X, and love, and everything, I didn't really understand what I was feeling."

Oh.

Now I get it. Matthew's X has finally been activated, as a direct result of OUR science project. But not even the Oracular Forces of All-Knowingness could have predicted that Matthew's X, once awakened, would end up pointing straight at JESS!

Bitter, bitter hindsight! Better to have let sleeping Dawg X lie. Too late now, though.

"I know she's your friend, so I don't have to tell you how great she is," Matthew goes on. "And I don't think she's interested in me, anyway. At least, it doesn't seem like she is. But until now I didn't know how . . . you know . . ." He trails off, the agony written all over his face.

"How wonderful and horrible it would feel?" I offer. "How endlessly you would think about it? How completely it would ruin your life?"

"Uh, yeah," he mumbles. "So I was thinking, now that I understand this crush thing a little better, that maybe you might be mad at me."

"I'm not," I lie, again. I feel a tiny flash of pity for his suffering, which I squelch immediately. Squelch!

"That's good," he says. "Because I wanted to ask you something. About Jess."

How short the road from love to hurt! From rejection to revenge! One bleeds into the other as smoothly as a Creamsicle morphs from orange to vanilla.

Matthew Dwyer, the Dawg I Once Loved, has rolled in the poison ivy of unrequited X. I feel his pain, and I want him to suffer even more.

"Do you think," he says, turning his attention to the pepper mill. "Do you think I should–tell her?"

Knowing, as I do, the full extent of Jess's lack of interest in Matthew, I do not hesitate even for a sliver of a split second. "Absolutely," I say.

If I were a cartoon I'd be sprouting little devil horns right now. How badly I want him to know what it's like to have your tender, heartfelt confession of love fall on indifferent ears! That's data he doesn't have yet.

"Really?" he says, his foolish heart quivering with hope. "What would she–I mean, YOU know her really well. What do you think she'll say?"

I lean very close to Matthew, not caring about my breath, because I am wrapped in a cloud of sulfur and brimstone. "Just tell her how you feel," I advise. "It's best to be open about these things."

The next day at the Pound, Ms. Blank hands me a fax from Berlin.

Dear Felicia,

I will be staying in Berlin until further notice. The reason, I am happy to tell you, is love.

But first, Berlin! A glorious place. The quality of the light, the music and the food! The setting is so very conducive to romance—all that was required was a suitable Fräulein.

Enter Miss Elke Wolfgram, whom I met at the award ceremony for my poems at the Deutsche Oper. There, with the cool night air lit by crystal chandeliers, filled with music by the Berlin Philharmonic, and attractively perfumed by Miss Wolfgram herself, a spark ignited that continues to burn, even as we get to know each other, haltingly, through her passable English and my impossible German.

At my age, when love comes, we must not ask foolish questions but seize the day and be glad.

I ask your forgiveness for my long absence, but perhaps something in this turn of events contains a lesson of relevance: about the universal language of love, the spell cast by a great city, or a different subject altogether. I leave the unpuzzling of all that to you, my dear Felicia.

For now, I will enjoy my Fräulein and look forward to your correspondence. Till next we meet, Ich bin ein Berliner!
Yours,
Frasconi

" *'Ich bin ein Berliner.'* President Kennedy said that," says Trip, turning to Deej. "Know what it means? 'I am a jelly donut.' "

Deej looks at him, supremely dubious. Trip, Deej, Jess, and I are in the math room, a box of Krispy Kremes on the table in front of us, our math books pushed to one side. Kat and Dmitri are rehearsing in the basement. I don't know where Randall is, but Matthew and Jacob are upstairs in the lab, trying to teach the rabbits to distinguish between a dozen or so of the more popular ragas in Indian classical music.

Little twangs from Jacob's sitar are audible through the ventilation system as Trip picks up a jelly-filled donut to illustrate his point. *"Ich bin ein Berliner!"* he says, and bites down. The jelly squirts everywhere and Trip guffaws at his own mess.

"Actually, that's a myth," I say, in the interests of accuracy, and also to conceal my disappointment over Mr. Frasconi's letter. "Though it's true that a Berliner is a jelly donut, in Germany." There's a whole section about conspiracy theories in my mom's bookstore, so I'm pretty well informed about JFK trivia. "In context, *'Ich bin ein Berliner'* means 'I'm one of you, I feel your pain,' that kind of thing." How could Mr. Frasconi abandon me like this. Falling in love? At his age? More ridiculous than a thousand foolish valentines.

"I get it. Like, I'm down with the peeps of Berlin," says Trip.

Deej looks at him, her eyes the color of the chocolate filling inside a chocolate-cream-filled Krispy. "You sound wack talking like a homey, Trip," she says, a glint of fun in her voice. "Because you are the whitest whiteboy I have ever seen!"

Trip laughs so hard he almost falls off his chair. "I'm just trying to fulfill my second-language requirement for college," he says. "But whiteboy and homey won't do it, huh?"

"No way," snorts Deej. "My grandma, Miss Doris, she's all proper, right? She's always on me and my cousins about the way we talk with each other. 'Doris Jean, you are an AFRICAN girl!" That's what Miss Doris says. 'You show your best manners where-EVAH you go.' " Deej makes a face. "But if I talk like Princess White Bread at my school–"

"They think you's buggin'?" says Trip, grinning.

"You got THAT right!" laughs Deej.

"Hey, Deej," Jess says, her bright-idea lightbulb twinkling on. "You're giving me a great idea! Standard English is a REALLY useful skill, I mean in terms of taking the SAT, future employability, and so on. Do you think we should incorporate some speech training into the peer tutoring program at your school next year?"

"Standard ENGLISH? Sku me, shorty!" Deej sounds rather miffed. "Do you think we don't get the network news on 145th Street?"

And then, in pitch-perfect, rapid-fire newscaster speech, every vowel and consonant plucked straight from the middle of mainland, strip-malled, and cineplexed America, Deej recites:

"In tonight's State of the Union address, the President will explain the state of the union, since we're too stupid to figure it out for ourselves! Full coverage of the white man's speech at eight, with more white men providing commentary at eleven! All this, plus sports, weather, and a special investigative report on Who-Put-This-Stick-up-My-Butt! Thank you for watching Caucasian News Network!"

That does it. Trip is now on the floor, with actual tears of laughter rolling down his cheeks.

And Jess, for once, is speechless, in every language.

Deej fixes Jess with her chocolate-cream stare. "At my school, we talk like we do because that's OUR slang. Like you and your friends got YOUR slang, like your Kitten-and-Dawg 'thang.' "

Jess's cheeks are so red right now I'm afraid she might cry. "You are totally right," she says. "That was utterly stupid of me, Deej. I apologize."

"It's okay, Jessie," Deej says, her tone softening. "Miss Doris says the same thing as you, about college and all. At Miss Doris's house we talk whiter than Trip!" Deej kicks Trip under the table, cracking him up all over again.

"I would LOVE to meet Miss Doris sometime," says Jess, starting to sound like herself again. "May I?"

"Me too," says Trip, weak from laughter, as he climbs back into his chair. "I bet she's a cool lady."

"Then I'm coming, too!" I say. "If we're invited, of course!"

"Y'all wanna meet my grandma?" asks Deej, looking at us in a you-people-are-crazy kind of way. "Oh, she is gonna love that!" Deej winks at Jess and smiles. "Miss Doris would LOVE to get a look at you, Jessica Kornbluth!"

Miss Doris is not the only person who would enjoy getting a look at Deej's new friends. That becomes clear the next afternoon, when Deej's former crew shows up at the Pound.

"Oh man, this is not good," mutters Deej when we walk out of school and see a small but raucous crowd of girls hanging out on Gramercy Park South.

It's one of those early April jacket-season days that fashion-conscious New Yorkers live for. Resplendent in our attractively layered outfits, Jess, Randall, Trip, Deej, and I are on our way to meet Matthew and Jacob and even hardworking Kat for a picnic in Madison Square Park. I'm looking forward to it—the chance to lie on the grass and stare at the clouds while dispensing coy, data-gathering tidbits of flirtiness to Randall and Observing his reactions. Not to mention the fun of watching Matthew squirm and suffer around Jess. He hasn't confessed his looooooove to her yet, despite my nefarious encouragement, but he's been looking pale and thin lately, with dark circles under his eyes.

"Can't we just wave and keep walking?" says Jess warily. Of the three black-eyed Kittens, Jess's eye has taken the longest time to heal.

"Relax," says Trip, puffing up his chest. "I think I can take a bunch of cute girls."

"Don't play around, Trip," warns Deej. "These girls are no fools and they have mean boyfriends. Let me go see what's up."

She walks up to them and puts her hands on her hips. "Yo Shally. Yo D'Neece."

"Why, Doris Jean! Look at your pretty new school!" the one called Shally teases her. "That is one fine house you got there. They make you clean it?" The half-dozen or so girls behind her bust out laughing at that one.

"Shut up, now," Deej says, perfectly friendly. "I am

so impressed you found your way here. You must've got yourself a map or something."

"Subway runs uptown AND down, or did you forget that already?" D'Neece says. "Now come on, tell us about private school! You meet any rich whiteboys yet?"

Deej is laughing, but she's nervous, I can tell. "These are my friends," she says, glancing at us and then back at Shally and D'Neece. "We're gonna go eat now, y'all coming or not?"

A loud conversation ensues over whether we should eat, what we should eat, where we should eat. Deej manages to introduce all of us by name, and though Jess and Shally pretend they've never met before, it's clear they have. Everybody's talking at the same time, but at least nobody's fighting.

Until these two sourpuss grown-up guys come strolling down Gramercy Park South.

"This is Gramercy Park. It's private. It's a quiet neighborhood," one of them barks. "Go fight somewhere else."

The volume of the group doubles as several girls answer at once.

"If you want privacy then stay home!"

"We're not fighting, we're talking!"

"If we were fighting you'd know it!"

Then the other guy says the stupidest, stupidest thing.

"So go talk somewhere else," he says. "Go back uptown, where you belong."

Now everybody starts yelling, but Deej's voice soars over the din.

"Excuse me, mister," says Deej. Shally and D'Neece

are flanking her like Charlie's Angels. "There is NO need for that kind of talk."

"It makes you sound like a racist bigot, for one thing," says Trip, stepping right next to Deej. "That kinda thinking is just unhip, dude."

Everybody gets quiet. I see Shally mouthing the words "rich whiteboy" to D'Neece, who looks impressed.

"Unhip?" snorts the guy, turning his full attention to Trip. "And what are you, a fag?"

"What if I was?" says Trip, locking eyes with him.

"You kids don't belong here. I'm calling the cops," says the first guy, taking out his phone.

"Call anyone you want. Just don't be rude to my friends," Trip says, as cool as I've ever seen anyone be.

All at once, like a flock of pigeons taking off in answer to some mysterious, prearranged signal, the crowd forms a circle around Trip and the Unhip Dude.

"Randall!" I say, in an urgent whisper. "Do something!"

Randall is standing in the relaxed, alert posture I recognize from the dojo, but he doesn't move. "Trip's got street smarts," he answers, watching. He takes a slow, deep breath. "Let him deal with these jerks."

But I'd seen enough cheesy cop shows on television to get myself all worked up. "He's on parole, remember?" I blurt. "If the police come, he could be in trouble or something!"

Without looking away from Trip, Randall shakes off the geeky oversized wristwatch he always wears and hands it to me. He pushes up his sleeves. "Don't tell my sensei," he murmurs, so only I can hear. "But I kind of always wanted to get into a fight."

Before I can say *bonne chance,* Randall is in the middle of the circle where Trip is facing off with the Unhip Dude. "What are you, the baby brother?" the guy says to Randall, starting to act all pumped. "The boyfriend?"

"Just a concerned, law-abiding citizen," says Randall, stepping in front of Trip. "But there's no law against idiots, unfortunately."

At the word "idiots," the guy reaches back and throws his first punch. Hard.

Exactly forty-five seconds after that punch is thrown, Randall and I are standing together on Gramercy Park South, doing something in front of everyone that I never, ever dreamed I'd be doing at all.

But wait! I am getting ahead of myself here! What happens is this:

No matter how the guy tried to hit him, Randall side-stepped it. The punch would come, and all of a sudden Randall was just, elsewhere, like he was zapped by Captain Kirk's transporter beam and rematerialized a few feet away. The guy was wearing himself out swinging. Randall looked almost bored. The crowd was going wild and rapidly growing, as students from the Pound crossed the street to check out the fight. And Deej was hanging on to Trip for dear life, trying to keep him out of it.

But when the other guy, the one who had called the cops, started to sneak up on Randall from behind, and no one seemed to notice but me, that's when this Kitten started to see red.

This Kitten experienced, for the first time in her life, what is meant by the term "ferocious clarity."

I mean, come on! Two against one? That is just not fair.

"Keeeee—YAH!" I scream, totally unthinking, running and leaping onto the second guy's back. I lock my arms around his neck and kick furiously. This succeeds in knocking him off balance, if nothing else. He falls to the side, on top of me. My head whacks the pavement. I'm seeing stars, and not the Hollywood kind, as sheer momentum rolls us over each other, till I end up on top. "Don't move," I holler in the guy's face. And I pray he doesn't, since I have no idea what to do next.

But he's not moving. He's not even looking at me. He's too busy watching his friend get an ass-whupping from the Randinator.

It seems the distraction of my rabid Kittenattack breaks Randall's focus for a half-second, giving his opponent an opening to land a punch. Which is unfortunate, since it leaves Randall no choice but to make physical contact. He swats the guy's oncoming fist away like a fly, grabs his arm, and flips him neatly over his shoulder. The Unhip Dude lands on his back with a thud. At which point Randall gently places one foot on the guy's throat.

"Sorry 'bout that," he says to the panting, bewildered Dude on the ground. "I think you two should leave now."

I'm vaguely aware of many Free Children gathered around, all whooping and cheering. But that's floating somewhere distant, far, far away from my pounding head, as I wobble to my feet. Someone is helping me up but I don't notice who it is until he speaks.

"That was incredibly brave," says Randall as he pushes my tangled hair out of my face. "Are you okay?"

And, okay. I freely admit what happens next.

I can offer no logical explanation, but I kiss him.

I kiss Randall, in front of everyone.

As I do, something electrical-feeling zaps through me, from the top of my messed-up hair all the way down to the tips of my chunky-heeled boots.

There is a fresh round of whooping and hollering from somewhere close by.

"Mutual Rescue!" I mumble to Randall, amazed. "I think I broke your watch."

"We better get you some ice," says Randall, who understands that I'm talking gibberish because I may have a concussion. He must have been surprised by the kiss. He didn't seem to mind it, though.

Just to make sure, I kiss him again. This time he's not surprised, and he definitely doesn't mind.

"I'm fine," I say.

I'm X-cellent, in fact!

14

A Clue from Mr. Frasconi, a Letter from Dmitri, and a Serious Talk with Randall

PARTY ON THE BOAT! PARTY ON THE BOAT!

Trip says we're having a party. What are we celebrating? Randall's vanquishing of the Unhip Dude, Deej's new friends (that's us!) making peace with her old friends, the arrival of spring, the phases of the moon, whatevah! But his dad's boat is docked downtown with a full crew and available for sunset circumnavigations round this island we call home, so Trip says it's time for a party on the boat. Formal, no less!

PARTY ON THE BOAT!

But before the cruisewear shopping commences, here's the rest of what happened on the day of the Great

Vanquishing, as it shall be passed down in legend and song: hail, hail, O Randall the Brave, with an assist from Ferocious Felicia!

By the time the cops arrive, the two Unhip Dudes are long gone (if Randall's ass-whupping wasn't sufficient motivation, the verbal encouragement offered by Shally and D'Neece, pissed-off and scary-faced as two teenage Terminatrixes, would make any sane man flee in terror). However, there is still a crowd of whooping and hollering kids outside Gramercy Park.

The patrol car arrives with lights flashing. A cop struts out, hand hovering rather near his billy club.

"Somebody in a fight?" he yells. "Who was in a fight?"

Laughter, pointing; the crowd parts like the Red Sea. Not Moses, but Randall steps forward.

My Randall! Who's fourteen but passes for twelve, who looks like he'd have to take steroids to win a chess tournament.

The look on the cop's face changes from stern to concerned when he sees the Baby-Faced Randinator.

"You okay, son?" he asks.

"Fine," says Randall mildly. "Nothing happened, really. Just some mean guys trying to scare us."

The cop surveys this happy group of teens celebrating a home-team victory on the south side of Gram. "Who are you kids?" he asks, suspicious.

"We're all friends, that's who," laughs Deej, twining one arm around Jess's neck and the other around Shally's.

"Right," says the cop. "And where do you and your friends go to school?"

Deej looks back and forth between her two pals. In her Princess White Bread newscaster voice, she replies, "East Harlem Academy, and I'm also a visiting student at the Manhattan Free Children's School, Officer, which is right across the street. They're both highly educational institutions! These are some of my classmates."

And Trip, who could easily be forgiven for wanting to fade into the crowd at such a moment, walks right up to the officer and sticks out his hand. "Harold Johnston Mathis the Third, sir! How do you do?"

"I'm fine, Harold, just fine," says the officer, his adrenaline level sinking back to normal. "Ten syllables or less, tell me what happened so I can get back to work."

"We were accosted by two small-minded gentlemen, who've moved on of their own accord," answers Trip. He's quite a few syllables over but the cop doesn't seem to care. "It's a shame people can't always get along in a great city like this. We're just heading out for some refreshments now. Care to join us?"

This is the place where you could insert some generic cops-eating-donuts joke.

Or this is the place where you could Observe that Matthew and Jacob and Kat got tired of waiting at Madison Park and came back looking for us, arriving just in time to see me in X-powered lip-lock with Randall, and half the Pound cheering us on.

Consequently, you could Describe the various looks on their faces, the O-shaped mouths, the cartoonish expressions of surprise. You could also mention the strange lump of satisfaction that formed in my chest when, still breathless from the kiss, I turned my face away from

Randall's and made brief, accidental eye contact with Matthew.

But there is a far more urgent question burning in my Kittenbrain, and that question is this:

Am I hooked up with Randall? Or not?

The Mutual Rescue worked better than anyone could have expected, and I extend all due props to Miss Dervish Greenstream for the tip. But is it enough? Will it last? I review what I've learned so far about X, and I plot the data points against the Randall-plus-me equation, but the answer is far from clear.

First of all, there's no Romeo/Juliet Thing. Nobody's trying to keep us apart.

We are not really opposites. In fact, Randall and I both tend toward the geeky and are prone to unrequited crushes. So we're more similar than not, much as I hate to admit it.

And yes, the Mutual Rescue worked major X-mojo, but it would be difficult, not to mention painful, to reenact that on a regular basis.

What else is there? Think, Felicia, think!

The setting . . .

so very conducive to romance . . .

Ich bin ein Berliner. . . .

That's it! The Romantic Setting.

Thanks, Mr. Frasconi!

But Randall and I don't have to go to Berlin, because Saturday night we'll be hangin' and chillin' in the most Romantic Setting evah! A sunset cruise on Trip's dad's boat. What could be more perfect?

I resolve to go all out: wear something girly, sneak a spritz of my mom's perfume, beg Kat to bring her violin.

Because the power of the Romantic Setting must not be squandered, and let's face it: Randall is smart, brave, open with his feelings, and capable of boyfriend-like behavior. And he likes me.

If I didn't notice Randall's X-cellent qualities before, was it only because I was wearing Matthew-blinders?

Matthew Dwyer, who is many, many wonderful things. But boyfriend-like is not among them.

"A *boyfriend*"—I hear my mother's voice, reverbever-beverberating in my head like a gong—"a *boyfriend* is NOT the only golden road to happiness!"

Yeah, well, she only says that because she doesn't have one.

Maybe my mom doesn't want a boyfriend. Or maybe she just can't find one.

But that doesn't mean I can't.

I thought Kat had summoned us to the Moonbeam to plan outfits for the party on the boat, but I thought wrong.

Her violin case is on the seat next to her, but tough Violin Kat, swearing-in-Russian Kat, get-out-of-my-way-or-I'll-stab-you-with-this-bow-Kat is nowhere to be seen. Instead, it's a defeated and totally heartbroken Kat who sits here in our favorite booth, sobbing. She pushes a piece of paper across the table to me and Jess. It's a letter, scrawled in teeny-tiny letters.

Dear Miss Katarina,

I have made terrible, terrible mistake. I write you this letter so you can please forgive me.

You are very serious person, and tall, and the language

you say when you practice violin is like grown man! Like angry sailor! I never think a teenage girl to say such things. And that is why my mistake. Katarina, I think you grown woman!

When you say we rehearse at "school," I say, yes, you are music teacher. When you tell me you have boyfriend, my heart break but that is life. Then the little boy comes. Your student, yes? But when he call you honey, baby doll, I see he is boyfriend of which you told me!

Only then do I realize you are high school girl!

Every time I see you for practice, I am full with humiliation to remember my idiot mistake. To think I wrote such words of love to a child!

Forgive me. I cannot recital with you. I cannot appear in public with this shame in my heart. You are talented girl. Use no more the dirty words, they are not for your girlish lips.

And be careful, dear Katarina. I think your little boyfriend is too much possessive. You shall "play the field," yes? That is what the young people do in America.

Forgive again for my advice but you are like baby sister to me now—
Dmitri

"It's over," Kat moans. "All that work. Wasted! Argosy Records, ruined! Everything's ruined."

She puts her head on the table and pounds her fist. Jess and I each grab our milk shakes before they spill.

"Why? Why can't everything happen the way it's supposed to? Why why why why why?" Kat laments, not caring if the whole Moonbeam hears.

I have a split-second vision of her dad on his wedding

anniversary, wailing and clutching a glass of vodka. It must be something to see.

"Kat," says Jess delicately. "It's really awful. But at least he apologized, isn't that one positive thing? It was all just a mistake."

"Why why why why why?" is what comes out, muffled and damp.

"Do you HAVE to have an accompanist?" I ask. I know it's a dumb question, but the scientific method has taught me not to take the obvious for granted. "I mean, I know that's how it's usually done, but—do you have to?"

Kat looks up at me, red eyed, wet cheeked. "What do you mean?" she growls. "A classical recital program, *solo*? That's insane! It's crazy, nobody does that! That's *bleep bleep bleepsky bleeping BLEEP!*" She hurls this last stream of profanity at Dmitri's letter.

"We're just trying to HELP, Kat!" chides Jess. "We have like, four whole days to solve this problem. You can't give up!"

"So what do you suggest?" Kat asks bitterly.

Jess smiles her Joan of Arc smile. I hear her mental binder snapping open to a new, freshly tabbed section. "For starters," she says, sounding unstoppably efficient, "I think I should talk to Dmitri."

"We need to talk," says Randall.

Uh-oh. This can't be a good sign.

Randall and I, on our first maybe-we're-hooked-up-now excursion, are strolling through the famed arch at Washington Square Park, where Fifth Avenue screeches

to a halt and the party called Greenwich Village officially begins.

"What did you mean by mutual rescue?" asks
Randall. "That's what you said to me, remember? Right
before we–before you–you know."

Mutual Rescue! I did say that. Is that what's worry-
ing him?

"Oh, that's nothing," I say. I wonder if we should be
holding hands. Isn't that what girls and their boyfriend-
like boyfriends do when they walk in the park? "Mutual
Rescue, it has to do with the science fair project I've
been working on."

"With Matthew?" he asks quickly. "That's the one
about your crush, right? The Search for X?"

Okay, now *je comprends tout.* He's worried that I still
like Matthew. How cute! How boyfriend-like! "My crush
on Matthew is over," I say, quite convincingly. "We have
this science project to finish, but we're just friends. In
fact," I say, feeling a little gossip-guilt but wanting to
offer as much reassurance as I can, "I know who
Matthew really likes!"

"I do, too," he says. "He's one of my best friends, remember?"

Whoops. So all that time I was mooning over
Matthew, Randall knew it was hopeless and respected
my feelings anyway. Huh. Another mental point
awarded to the Randinator.

Randall stops walking. "I wanted to be sure you
meant it," he says, plain and simple. "When you kissed
me. That you weren't just trying to make Matthew jealous or something."

Silly Randall. Silly, silly, silly Randall. As if I would do something like that. As if.

"I wasn't," I say. I take Randall's hand. It's smooth and warm. Fingers entwine. He smiles at me and tucks our joined hands into his jacket pocket.

But was I?

Matthew&Felicia . . .

2-gethah . . .

4-evah . . .

Shaddup, already! The Love Boat sails tomorrow. The Romantic Setting is on its way. Just gotta hang on till then—

"Hey, George," says Randall. "How ya doin', George?"

The Washington Arch features not one, but two statues of George Washington. On the east pillar is Washington at war; on the west, Washington at peace. I'm facing the eastern statue, and for a second it looks like the Father of Our Country is heaving a big, exasperated sigh, aimed right at me.

You think winning independence from the British was hard? I want to say to him. Try overthrowing the tyranny of X!

King George III was a pussycat compared to this!

By rights New York City should have at least another week or two of spring, but by the next day, Saturday, the climate has prematurely shifted, in a worrisome, global-warming kind of way into hot and humid no-coat season. At least, on dry land it has.

"Bring a sweater," my mom says. "It's always chilly on the water." I take this as the best possible sign. It may be no-coat weather in the city, but it's always jacket season at sea. No wonder the rich buy boats.

And the et sweatera idea is perfect, because the dress I finally decided on is a groovy retro halter-top number, a satiny green so dark it's almost black, with a wide pleated sash and full skirt—only eighteen bucks at the vintage clothing store down the street from the Unbound Page. A pair of black kitten heels—that's what they're called, really!—a pretty black lambswool sweater and a beaded clutch purse from my mom's bottomless closet, and I am a vision.

Mom walks me downstairs and makes the surprising and extravagant gesture of springing for a taxi. "You look much too pretty to take the bus," she says, sticking her arm in the air. A yellow chariot pulls up almost instantaneously.

"Bon voyage!" says Mom, tucking the cab fare into my purse and taking one last look at me in my glamour getup. She carefully pinned me in so the halter bra won't shift around and show straps. She also helped with my hair, which is piled up on my head and sprayed into perfect immobility.

"Felicia, honey," Mom says, "you are developing a very nice figure."

Furball alert canceled, at least for tonight. "Thank you," I say, and then whisper in her ear, "I must get it from you, hotsy mama!" She laughs, and I think the old girl even blushes a little. I smooch her on the cheek and climb into the cab.

"North Cove Yacht Harbor, please," I say, oh-so-elegant. "By Battery Park. I have a boat to catch."

15

The Fourth Experiment Leaves Us All at Sea, as Kittens and Dawgs Get Shipwrecked by the Most Fearsome X Mojo of All!

The very first person I run into at the North Cove Yacht Harbor is Matthew. He is gorgeous. Correction: The sky above New York Harbor is a tropical Hawaiian blue, the late-afternoon sun sends long, sparkling tendrils of light stretching across the water like diamond-studded taffy, the pristine gazillion-dollar yachts bob up and down like happy pampered pets, the breeze is cool and smells of salt and men's cologne. Careful, I tell myself as he approaches, inoculating my heart against the X-forces that eddy around us, invisible and all-powerful. It's the Romantic

Setting that's heart-stoppingly gorgeous, not Matthew, Matthew is exactly the same as he ever was. . . .

"Wow, Felicia," he says, sounding stunned. "You look beautiful!"

Why why why why why? I lament inwardly. Why am I here to woo Randall, and Matthew to woo Jess, when all along it was supposed to be me and him? Him and me?

But "play it cool" will be my motto for the evening, because the Romantic Setting has us in its clutches already, and we've got a whole island to boogie round before the night is through. I adjust my sunglasses against the glare and nod my thanks, smiling my best Italian-movie-star half-smile.

"Which one of these rowboats is Trip's?" I ask wittily.

"All of them!" proclaims Trip, appearing behind us in a flawless white linen suit. "But I recommend—this one."

Trip gestures across the marina, to the prettiest, not to mention biggest, yacht that's moored in the whole North Cove. "The *Betty Johnston!*" he says. "She's the apple of my daddy's eye. Do I mean my mom, or the boat? I'll let you decide! Betty, Junior, meet my friends."

Alors! The gazillionaire and his wife! Snatches of the *Gilligan's Island* theme song play in my head. The Mathises look like people you'd see in a magazine. Fit, tan, with beautiful clothes. Trip's mom has an actual gauzy kerchief tied around her upswept hair. Talk about Italian movie star! It's the most glamorous thing I've ever seen.

"My dear!" exclaims Betty to me. "Aren't you delicious! What a knockout dress. I had one exactly like it when I was your age!" Her laugh tinkles like bells. I could tell her, if I weren't so star-struck by her fabulousness, that if she's in the habit of donating her old clothes to thrift shops there's a good chance this IS her dress.

Junior shakes Matthew's hand. Trip is shielding his eyes from the sun, scanning the crowds on the marina.

"Hey!" Trip yells. "Over here!" He's waving, and after a moment we see at whom. It's Deej. She's skittering across the plaza in sky-high lemon-colored heels, looking every which way for Trip's voice and giving her dress one final, perfecting tug in back before returning his wave. Her outfit is da bomb, her cocoa-cinnamon skin set off by a creamy yellow sheath. Her hair, usually pulled straight back and slicked against her head, is wrapped up high in a boldly patterned scarf, Egyptian goddess–style. Total effect: teen-supermodel love child of Nefertiti and Jackie Onassis. Her smile, when she sees Trip, is dazzling.

"Harrrrrold," she purrs, running up and giving him a peck on the cheek. "I got stuck on that downtown train, I was afraid I was gonna miss the boat!" She turns and sees me. "Whooo, F'leesha!" she cries, delighted. "You are looking fine!"

"Mother, Dad, this is my special friend, Doris Jean," says Trip. "The young lady I told you about."

"The exchange student?" asks Betty, carefully, not revealing for a heartbeat that perhaps she had been expecting a shy Swiss heiress who skis with her father, the ambassador, on school holidays and summers at the family home in Majorca.

"Visiting student is what they call it. Mr. and Mrs.

Mathis, I am so very happy to meet you!" exclaims Deej, with charm to spare. "And please call me Deej. It's a nickname, but it's what I go by. My grandma's name is Doris, like mine, so they gotta call me something or nobody can tell who's talking to who."

"I sympathize completely!" says Harold "Junior" Mathis. "Every man in my family is named Harold. We've been through Hal, Harry, Hardy—finally we gave up and started using numbers, so I go by Junior and my son here got stuck with Trip."

"It suits him," says Deej, giving her Special Friend a sweet nudge.

"Because so often he *is* one, don't you find?" laughs Betty.

Deej giggles and slips her slender arm through Trip's. "You and Deej will have dinner with us, I hope?" says Betty to her son. "Captain's table, you can't refuse!"

"Of course, Mom. Have I told you lately you're a peach?" Trip takes his mother's arm and the three of them, elbows linked, saunter together toward the boat named after Betty, laughing in perfect three-part harmony: tinkling soprano, jazzy alto, and roughened but still boyish tenor.

The bass of this quartet, Junior, has stopped to light a cigar. He stands on the marina, smoking, and Matthew and I walk past him as we approach the boarding ramp of the *Betty Johnston.*

"Thanks so much for having us, Mr. Mathis," I say. "This is amazing."

Trip's dad exhales a fragrant puff, politely aiming it away from me. "You're all such nice kids, I can see that already," he says, his voice sounding strangely gruff. "It makes me gladder than you can possibly know."

Matthew and I smile and start to move on, but Mr. Mathis abruptly turns back to us. "Don't ever think there are no second chances," he says, hoarse and urgent. "Of course there are. That's all life is, one second chance after another after another." He blows out another puff. "Thank God."

I hear it now. It's not the smoke that's making his voice gruff. He's actually choked up.

"Thank you," I say again. And Matthew and I step on board the Love Boat.

Randall's already there, milling about the lower deck near the ramp. It's sweet that he's waiting for me, but it also means he sees me arriving with Matthew. And what of it? I can't help it if we happened to show up at the same time, and it was, honestly, pure coincidence, even though I don't usually believe in coincidences.

"Hey," he says with a nervous smile. I have to say, this Romantic Setting mojo is unbelievable. I've never seen Randall looking so swell. In fact, I've scarcely noticed how Randall looks before, even when I was kissing him. But tonight he is a handsome, lean, and light-footed Dawg in a chocolate brown suit and colorful striped tie. He's had a haircut, too, and his thick black hair is kind of spiked and hipster-looking. There may be hair product involved. In sum, Randall is a cupcake.

"You look fantastic," he says, taking my hand.

"You too," I say, meaning it.

"Hey, buddy!" says Matthew. "Cool boat, right?"

"Awesome. You gotta see the upstairs, the whatever-it's-called—"

"Crow's nest?"

"No, that's only in pirate ships, dude!"

"Oh man! Think we'll see any pirates?"

And so the happy Dawg banter begins. I long to see Jess and Kat and check out their fab outfits, so I excuse myself from inspecting the *Betty J* with the Dawgs and wander onto the main deck. I spot Kat on the upper level, gazing moodily out to sea. She's wearing a long-sleeved, high-necked, loose-fitting, black shroud, I guess you could call it, but she looks gorgeous anyway, pale and severe. I see Jacob up there, too, looking right at home on a private yacht, which is not surprising considering his famous Mother Thespian and all.

Then, on the far side of the main deck, across from where I'm standing, I spot an adorable auburn-haired Kitten who's wearing, get this, practically the same dress as me. Not exactly the same, because mine is a halter top and Jess's has cap sleeves with a heart-shaped neckline. And hers is actually a navy blue, so dark it's almost black, but unless you're standing in bright light you can hardly tell the difference.

We hug and squeal about the dresses. I'm about to joke that Trip's mom must have given away a lot of clothes over the years, but Jess beats me to the conversational punch.

"I brought a guest!" she says.

Is her older brother home from the Peace Corps? I can't imagine who else she'd bring.

So I start to ask her, "Is your brother home from–" and then I see Jess's "guest."

Her brooding, tormented "guest," who's staring gloomily over the water, like Mr. April from the Depressed Russian Pianists pinup calendar.

"Uh, Jess?" I say, pulling her away to a private spot behind the lifeboats. I try not to sound like I think she's gone wacko. "What is Dmitri doing here?"

"Trip said we could bring a guest, so I did!" she says, all blithe and normal-acting. Well, yeah, but since all the Kittens and Dawgs were invited anyway, there was sort of no need to bring anyone. At least, that's what the rest of us, the NOT CRAZY people, had concluded.

"Dmitri . . . is . . . your . . . guest?" I want to give her time to really hear how mental this is.

"I'm trying to help Kat!" she chirps. "I want to show him how important it is that he NOT back out of her recital! She's SO upset about it!"

I glance up again at Kat, who does seem to be in mourning. Jess prattles madly, gaining speed as she goes. "Lucky that Trip's mother is on the board of Carnegie Hall, that's how I finally convinced him to come. Fee, it's perfect. We're on a *boat*! He HAS to hear me out, where else can he go? And Kat is going to play for everyone after dinner. Once he sees how incredible she is in performance, how AWFUL it would be if she had to cancel her recital . . ."

I hear Jess's words. They're fine words, all in perfect standard English. I just don't believe them. I say nothing. My dubious look speaks for itself.

"I was thinking of Kat! Really!"

My dubiousness is taking on intergalactic proportions. There has never been a more "I don't THINK so!" expression on anyone's face than there is on mine at this moment.

"You invited Dmitri," I say. She looks at me, the picture of innocence.

"To the party." She's still not cracking.

"On the BOAT?!!!"

They say every criminal wants to be caught, and this seems to be true of Jess, whose cheeks suddenly turn as pink as Johnny Depp's lips. "Ohmigod, Fee!" Jess says, the truth gurgling forth. "I know, I'm INSANE! But have you ever, ever, ever seen anything like him? EVER?"

"JESS! He's like, THIRTY!" We are struggling not to shout, since Dmitri is standing on the other side of the lifeboats.

"I KNOW! I know nothing will happen!" I watch, helpless, as Jess plunges the remaining distance into kookooland. "I just thought it would be amazing to hang out with him! Especially tonight! It's so–I mean, the water, and the sunset and everything. You know?"

Of course I know.

Jess, like the rest of us, is now helpless, captive, a willing victim of (insert Terrifying Horror-Movie Sound Track Music here)–

The Romantic Setting! *Aaaaaaaaaaaaaahhhhhh!*

The most fearsome X-mojo of all!

Dinner on the *Betty Johnston* makes the multi-ethnic gourmet fare at the Pound look like warmed-over Mickey D's. Five-star restaurant fare is one thing–what else would the Mathises offer, hardtack and scurvy pills?—but we are a tad surprised when champagne is served, since we know Trip is now a nondrinking kind of dude and the rest of us are, more or less, fourteen. But his parents are here so it must be okay, and we each take a little glass, even Trip. It is ultradelicious, bubbly and subtly flavored, like carbonated almond juice.

Dmitri doesn't stop at one glass, and the more he drinks, the more he seems to be pouring his heart out to Jess. The two of them are having a very intense-looking conversation. I send Jess a psychic message not to forget to argue Kat's case about the recital before her Kittenbrain gets completely boggled by Dmitri-X and champagne.

Trip and Deej are at one end of the table with Trip's parents. I'm sitting with Randall, and Kat has become the focal point of Jacob's gallantry, which she endures. And poor Matthew. The odd man out. Jess having an X-quake over Dmitri is a turn of events no one expected.

As for Cupcake Randall: he grows more boyfriend-like by the minute. He's charming and attentive, with a sly sense of humor. And he has awfully good manners. Not the medieval-courtier kind like Jacob, but just nice, like he always seems to notice when someone hasn't spoken for a while and makes a point of asking them a question. I like that.

The evening is going so well, in fact, that I'm starting to get nervous—no, worried—no, TERRIFIED that the major Romantic Setting X-mojo being generated right now on the Love Boat could spin out of control, ricocheting at crazy angles and zapping me back to a place I do not want to be. As the luscious desserts arrive (an elaborate ice cream concoction with bitter chocolate shavings and a single perfect boysenberry nestled on a geranium leaf), I resolve to be strong. The Romantic Setting may be powerful, but it's no match for the will of a Ferocious Kitten! If there is any Matthew-X left in my heart, now is the time to kibosh it.

Kibosh! I say to my heart. I spray a *pffft* of X-Be-Gone upon you!

As if hearing my thoughts and finding them ludicrous, at that very moment the swirling forces of X send Randall off to the little sailor's room, leaving an empty seat next to me, into which Matthew instantly slides.

"Hey," he says. "Great dessert. Did you know boysenberries were discovered by Rudolph Boysen? It's an interesting example of chance selection, a genetic cross between a blackberry and a raspberry. I wrote a paper on it once."

"No," I say, my heart giving a sideways lurch.

"Listen," says Matthew. "I was thinking about what we were discussing the other day. The Romantic Setting. Remember?"

Well, duh. I was hoping we could devise some benign, impersonal Romantic Setting experiment about the relative X-benefits of sixty-watt bulbs versus hundred-watt–

"Wouldn't you say this qualifies?" Matthew asks, looking around. "The mood, the food, the ambience? Have you noticed how we all seem much more attractive than we really are?"

"It's a Romantic Setting, no question," I mumble.

Come back, Randall, come back! I forbid myself to make eye contact with Matthew, since one look into those storm-colored depths might turn me to stone like a victim of Medusa, melt me into a puddle like the Wicked Witch of the West, make me leap onto the table and scream "I LOVE MATTHEW DWYER!" like F'Leesha losing her mind. Kibosh kibosh kibosh—

"I agree," says Matthew. "Which means our next experiment is going to happen—now." He sounds awfully sure of himself. I want to tell him, Look around. It's happening already, everywhere you turn.

He lowers his voice. "There will never be a better time for me to tell Jess that I like her. I'm gonna do it tonight. On the boat, in the Romantic Setting."

"Wow," I hear myself say. "What a great experiment."

Poor Matthew! Not only is Jess not interested in him, but right now her X-receptors are so clogged with Dmitri-X that not even Clearasil could help.

My mind races. What will happen when Jess says no thanks? Matthew's X, till now safely fixed on its target, will be suddenly cut free, like a kite that breaks its string. In a Romantic Setting like this it's bound to land somewhere. What if, even for a moment, even if only on the rebound, it bounces off ME?

Me, Felicia! Would I be able to resist a morsel of rebound X with Matthew, despite my budding boyfriend-bliss with Randall? Would I even try?

"But how will I ever get her away from that gross Russian guy?" Matthew ruminates. "He's talking her ear off."

I know that now is the time to tell him Jess is a lost

cause. Save him the heartbreak. I know what the right thing to do is. I open my lips to reply.

But my inner devil, perhaps wishing for just such a rebound effect to be put into play, overrules.

"I think I can help" is what I say.

"Oh, JESSica!" I croak a little while later, as I sidle over to where my X-addled Kittenpal is standing much too close to her never-gonna-happen fantasy man.

Dessert is *finis,* and Jess and Dmitri, with Randall and me tagging along, have gone upstairs to get some fresh air and check out the view. Lower Manhattan may be a forest of glass and steel, but the top of the island is a forest of actual trees, and the *Betty Johnston* is now passing through the narrow canal that separates Manhattan from the Bronx. Randall waves and hollers to the families having their sunset picnics on the grass and the kids playing softball on a waterfront field, but my chest is rapidly filling with guilt and I can hardly speak.

Here, right at the watery corner where the Harlem and Hudson rivers meet, as the East Side morphs into the West, we see the first stars of the evening twinkling over the Palisades.

"Randall, Jess and I are out of champagne!" I say, desperately exploiting my new status as one of the boyfriended. "Would you and Dmitri mind getting us some more?"

"I've had plenty, thanks," Jess says.

"We'd reallyreallyreally love some, thanks thanks THANKS!" I say, sounding loony. Randall gives my hand a squeeze and ushers Dmitri down the steps.

They're gone. "Jess," I begin. "We need to talk."

"What a life!" Jess sighs. "He's been telling me all about his terrible childhood, and the conservatory in Odessa, and coming to America, and the pain and torment and struggle. Gosh, it's FREEZING up here!" Jess rubs her bare arms, shivering.

It's always chilly on the water, for the innocent, but I feel hot and flushed. I lend Jess my black lambswool sweater. "Yes, he seems very brooding and tormented," I say nervously. "If he were fictional he'd be perfect for you. Listen, Jess–"

"You mean like Mr. Rochester?" Jess asks. "That's intriguing. OH! We talked about Kat's recital. Dmitri says–"

"Jess!" I interrupt. "Matthew really, really wants to talk to you."

She stares at me like I'm speaking a foreign language. "About what?"

Should I go through with my evil plan? Send Matthew to his romantic doom and hope to catch a little X on the rebound, or run back and tell him the truth, or what?

Out of the corner of my eye, I see something big and black dive-bomb out of the sky and smash into the water, emerging a moment later with a fat, waggling fish in its beak. It's way too big for a duck, too dark to be a seagull–it's just a really big, black bird, with a neat white cap on its head that looks weirdly familiar–

A bald eagle! There used to be hundreds of them living in the Hudson River Valley, till the river got too polluted. But now things are much better; the fish are running and the eagles are slowly coming back. Jess doesn't seem to notice it at all.

"You could mind your own beeswax!" says the eagle, landing on the railing of the *Betty J* with a slow flopping of its broad wings. The eagle has a strange but oddly compelling voice. Like a combination of my mom and Mr. Frasconi, but "beeswax" is definitely a Charles word–

"Who CARES whose voice it is?" says the eagle, spitting seawater and wrapping its curved claws around the rail. "I'm just saying, you could butt out of Matthew's X-business, wish him well, and get on with your life!"

Let go of my Matthew obsession FOR REAL and get ON with my LIFE? Easy for you to say, strange but compelling voice emanating from a bird!

"You have to admit," comments the fish, twisting around in the eagle's beak, "that obsessing about Matthew is not exactly the same thing as caring about Matthew."

"And what Matthew wants right now is the chance to lay his X on the table and roll the dice, risk his heart, and be fearless and foolhardy in the name of love," the eagle agrees.

"So if she REALLY cares about Matthew," reasons the fish, "shouldn't she help him take the risk he's ready to take?"

"Maybe," says the eagle. "Dunno, that's up to her."

"Ouch!" yelps the fish. "Careful with the beak!"

"Sorry!" says the bird. And then, very carefully, the eagle swallows his dinner and flies away.

Jess is still waiting for me to answer.

Breathe in, breathe out.

Apparently, there are some forces in the universe more powerful than one Kitten can understand or control, talking wildlife being one and the Romantic Setting being another. Who am I to say what might or might not happen if I stop scheming and obsessing and just step aside, letting the current and the tides, the moon's gravity and the salty breeze carry this Ship of Love where they may?

I make my decision. I take another deep breath and speak.

"Jess, Matthew REALLY likes you. And I think you should give him a chance."

"Fee, have you lost your MIND?" she almost shrieks. She is a fine one to talk about losing minds.

"Matthew is a great guy," I say, fast. We don't have much time. "He's smart and nice and he likes you. I think you should stop wasting your energy on this fantasy man and hear him out."

She stares at me. Is a light dawning in her eyes? I can't tell. "I really, truly mean it, Jess," I say.

And here comes Matthew. He's at the top of the stairs, right on cue.

Matthew Soon-to-Know-Heartbreak Dwyer! Full of tender hope, an X on his heart, his heart on his sleeve, the Kitten he loves in absurd infatuation with someone else.

I cross my fingers for him. Maybe the Romantic Setting X-mojo will prevail. Maybe a spark will fly between him and Jess. Maybe Dmitri will jump into the Hudson and swim back to Odessa.

Inwardly I wish Matthew luck, I truly do, and then,

before I start to cry, I dash away as fast as my kitten heels can carry me.

I want to make it clear that I didn't see any of what happened next. I didn't see Matthew's shy but earnest entreaties of love. Or Jess's kind, impatient face, or the way her eagerness to get back to Dmitri made her want to cut this short, so she took Matthew's hands in her own and leaned close to him, saying what a nice guy he was and that she valued him as a friend, but that's all.

And I didn't see how Matthew (who, let's face it, had never encountered this kind of data before) was not prepared for how shaky and upset her words made him feel, or how Jess, sorry for his pain, put her arms around him and gave him a long, supportive hug.

Jess, who's wearing my sweater, over her near-identical-to-mine dress, in the cool night air that's now lit only by stars. There is no moon tonight.

Nor did I see Randall watching all this in the semi-dark from the top of the stairs, a glass of champagne in each hand. (Dmitri had refused to come back up once he got down to the cabin. What Dmitri really wanted was to talk to Trip's mother about making his Carnegie Hall debut, and he'd simply been waiting for the champagne to kick in sufficiently to give him the courage to approach her. This had taken longer than expected, but now the time had come. Dmitri had forgotten all about Jess, who, let's face it, was just another precocious teenage girl to him.)

Of course, Randall couldn't hear what Jess and Matthew were saying, but he saw the hands taking hands, the leaning in close, the long, emotional embrace.

And all the while, he knew for certain it was me.

I had no idea any of this was happening, because I'm already back inside the cabin, trying to act normal, feeling hollow as a chocolate bunny but strangely relieved, too. The last of the coffee cups have been cleared, and Kat, after many entreaties from Junior, Betty, Trip, Deej, and Jacob, is taking out her violin. Dmitri is in the back of the cabin, looking pouty and cross.

(Only later would we learn that Trip's mother had gently refused his offer to audition for her right there, citing both the inappropriateness of the occasion and the lack of a piano on board the *Betty J* as reasons, and suggesting he send a tape and packet of press clippings to the program director's office at Carnegie Hall. Poor Dmitri found himself tangled in the Möbius strip of frustration all artists face: he had no reviews because he had not yet made his debut, and yet Carnegie would not consider him till he had reviews to send. Hence, his foul temper.)

Kat is ready to begin. Randall's not here, and I'm ashamed to say that for the moment I've forgotten all about him, because my mind is too busy trying not to think about Jess and Matthew, directly above us.

"Is that goth?" asks Betty, puzzled by Kat's somber attire.

"I think she's Amish," quips Trip.

"She is like Masha!" Dmitri blurts, a bit drunken-sounding, from the back of the cabin. "She mourns for her life! As we all should! *Bleepsky bleeping bleep!*" he exclaims, looking at our uncomprehending faces. "Do you not read Chekhov? *The Three Sisters?* Never will they get to Moscow! Never never never never never–"

Trip's dad moves next to Dmitri and talks to him quietly. Kat, eyes flashing, speaks. Her voice fills the cabin, strong and bitter as a double espresso.

"This piece was prepared for the most important recital of my life, which now cannot happen. Enjoy!"

And she launches, unaccompanied and with brooding torment, into her Rachmaninoff. I'm sure I hear Dmitri weeping by the end, but I don't dare look at him. We all clap like maniacs when she's done. She sits down, her point made.

"Brava!" yells Trip. "We have so much musical talent here tonight I don't know where to begin!" He turns to Deej. "How about a song, Deej?"

The rest of us clap and cheer, but Deej shakes her head, laughing, and covers her face. It's cute to see her being so shy.

"Maybe later!" Trip says, putting his hands on her shoulders. "Luckily for all of you, I seem to have misplaced my ukulele—"

"Boo! Boo!" we yell.

"So I'll go ahead and introduce—the amazing Shashti! You're on, Jake!"

Modestly, Jacob takes out his sitar and prepares to play. "This music can get really spiritual," he says as he gives the tuning pegs a twist. "So don't be surprised if you start seeing visions and whatnot. Just keep breathing and relax."

Duly warned, we breathe and relax, except for Kat, who is fascinated by the sitar and sits up quite straight, watching intently. I see Betty and Junior cuddling close. Trip sips more bubbly out of a fluted glass and wraps his arm around Deej. The way the two of them look at each other seems to give off actual sparks.

Jacob starts to play, and I let my eyes close so I can look for visions, but not a bird or a fish this time. A pony would be more fun. Anyway, it's magical, so magical that all of a sudden I wish I were holding hands with Randall. He'd love this.

But Randall is nowhere to be found.

Music, as Mr. Frasconi observed, is an essential component of the Romantic Setting. Which might explain why, after the impromptu concert is done and I wander the *Betty J* looking for Randall, I spot Kat and Jacob in a secluded spot on the main deck, holding hands and talking. I'm too far away to hear what they're saying, but my head is still swirling and it's easy to imagine their conversation:

"Your fingering is amazing, Shashti."

"Yours, too. And please call me Jacob."

"Don't you hate when you practice and practice and still make mistakes?"

"There are no mistakes."

"I hate memorizing."

"So don't. Improvise."

Whatever it is they're really saying, it's at that moment that Jacob leans forward in an unmistakably prekiss move.

Poor, poor Jacob. If only he had on a life preserver he might survive the unforgiving currents of the Hudson, which will soon consume him when Kat throws him overboard. But he's not wearing a life preserver, just a vintage suit jacket and narrow tie, and thus ends the promising career of a budding world musician. I dread to think of the histrionics that will ensue when Mother Thespian learns how Jacob met his watery end at the hands of an outraged violinist, and all because of X.

But what's this? Kat is not throwing Jacob overboard. She's not even screaming Russian swearwords at him.

I have to rub my eyes a minute.

They're making out.

Yup, Katarina No-Thanks-I'm-Allergic-to-Dawgs Arlovsky is making out with Shashti, I mean, Jacob, smooching *avec* tongue on the aft deck of the Love Boat, as one by one the stars turn up their twinkle power and the New Jersey Palisades fade to black in the west.

Bow down, O mortals, and tremble at the mighty X-power of the Romantic Setting!

As I make myself scarce, I could swear I see a shooting star high above New Jersey, drawing a happy exclamation point of light in the freshly darkened sky.

After the dinner spent watching the X-sparks fly off Trip and Deej (not to mention Junior and Betty, though theirs are dimmer sparks of the inferior grown-up variety, to my eye, at least), then the surprise of finding Kat and Jacob making an X-discovery of their own, and the effort of not thinking about the conversation that is none of my beeswax between Matthew and Jess, topped off with the mystery of the Disappearing Cupcake—add it up and I'm feeling a little lonesome and strange, loitering solo on the front deck.

The lights of the George Washington Bridge are

strung in a perfect arch, like a thousand fireflies in a meticulously planned aerial ballet. I'm watching the lights get closer and closer when Randall, furious, finds me.

"There you are!" I say, trying to sound happy and not all "Where the *bleepsky bleep* have you been?"

But Randall isn't here for chitchat. "Why couldn't you tell the truth?" he asks, as if I know what he's talking about. "I would have understood! But to pretend you liked me when you still like Matthew is just–mean! I was looking forward to tonight, Felicia, because I really liked you, and I still do, and now I feel awful!"

"What?" I say, bewildered. "What are you talking about?"

"I saw you together!" he cries. "You and Matthew! He's the one you really want, right? So what does that make me? Another one of your goofy experiments?"

I'm flabbergasted by how upset he is. Remember, I still don't know what he saw. I don't figure that out till the next day, when Jess comes by my apartment to give me back my sweater and we compare notes and start screaming.

But it doesn't matter, because right now Randall's standing here, totally upset with me, and there's more than a teaspoon of truth in his accusations.

"Randall," I say weakly. "I don't know what you mean. I've been in the cabin listening to Kat and Jacob play. And then I came out here looking for you."

And of course, that's when Matthew shows up, panting, wild-eyed, overflowing with feeling. He's almost unrecognizable.

"Felicia!" he says with passion. "There you are! I've been looking everywhere for you!"

The look on Randall's face is terrible.

Matthew sees his friend. "Hey, Randall," he ventures.

But Randall, with absolutely no reason to doubt the evidence of his own eyes, is gone.

Randall! I call, on the inside. But my voice is frozen.

Matthew doesn't notice, because he can't stop talking. "Listen! Felicia, I feel like I have to tell you this right now before I forget what it feels like. I did it! I talked to Jess, I was open, like you said. I said everything! I mean, I've never talked to anybody before in my whole life like that! In a way it was awful, because–"

"She said no," I say, tearing up. "I'm so sorry, Matthew. I knew she wasn't interested, it was mean of me not to tell you–"

"Wait-wait-wait," he says, wanting to finish. "In a way it was awful, and in a way it was, I don't know. Cool. Just to say all those things to someone, and have my heart totally break, and still be alive, the moment after. Here, in this beautiful place. Like getting a second chance, or something."

I wish I could follow his meaning, but I can't just now.

"So that's what I wanted to tell you," he concludes. "That's it." I nod, sniffling in time to the waves, a moist, improvised duet.

The lights of the bridge are getting very close now. Soon we'll be passing underneath.

"You–you knew she wasn't interested?" Matthew asks after a moment.

"I should have told you before," I say, sadder than sad. How can I explain? "But I was hoping your experiment might work."

Which I was, more or less, when I still had a boyfriend and wished similar joy on all the world. That was a long time ago, though.

"Oh," says Matthew, his euphoria slowly deflating like a dying balloon.

The lights of the bridge loom ahead. "How's Randall?" Matthew asks.

"Fine," I say, numb. "I think he just broke up with me."

"Oh," says Matthew. His mouth is O shaped. "Oh."

It's a long way round Manhattan by boat. There are no shortcuts. You can't cut across Central Park or change your mind in Midtown and hail a cab to take you home early.

So there's plenty of time to stare at the water, not talking, and think. Or to try with all your might not to think, of anything.

Matthew and I are alone on deck. Wherever Kat and Jacob are they're playing music again, but together this time. I can hear their intertwined melodies faintly on the wind.

Once upon a time, I would have dreamed this moment. Me and Matthew, in the starlight, music playing in the background. The surface of the Hudson shimmers around us, lapping out the rhythms of all the great love poems of the world against the hull of our own private Love Boat. Lovers embrace, fade-out and happy ending guaranteed.

"I guess the Romantic Setting was a bust," Matthew says, sounding glum. I know he's thinking of Jess.

"Guess so," I say, thinking of Randall's hurt face.

"Felicia," Matthew begins. It feels weird to hear him say my name. "You don't still have a crush on me, do you?"

I search my heart.

"Not really," I say. It's mostly true.

"Good," he says. "I hate to think you ever felt like I do now. It's awful."

"I know," I say.

But the Romantic Setting has a fearsome and powerful mojo and will not be mocked. As Matthew and I stand there, half in the shadow of the bridge, with a thousand twinkling fireflies above and New Jersey to the west, we are unmistakably standing much, much closer together than we typically do.

"Look at the George Washington Bridge," I say. It's above us, sparkling like a jeweled runway.

"Yes. The traffic is terrible," says Matthew, turning his head so it's very close to mine.

Then, powered by starlight, nudged closer by music, as if our lips thought of it themselves, we kiss.

His lips are dryer than I'd always imagined they would be. My heart is calmer. The kiss is sweet. My kitten heels remain strangely unmoved.

"That was nice," I say, reaching up and pushing his hair off his forehead, as I've so often longed to do. It falls back as soon as I move my hand away.

"I'm sorry about, you know," he says. "The way everything's turned out."

"Me too," I say, hiding in his arms against the salty wind that starts to kick up as we're standing there. Jess still has my sweater. "I am, too."

And I feel the last wisp of Matthew-X spread its wings and fly away from my heart, catching a ride on the salt breeze to who knows where.

That night I didn't even bother to tell my mom why, because it was too big to tell. But I crawled into the Murphy bed next to her and I cried and cried till I fell asleep. She kept stroking my sticky, sprayed hair and I think, before I actually conked out, that I might have heard her crying a little bit, too.

16

An Unexpected Switcheroo Is Our Fifth and Final Experiment

The Haiku of Why

Why why why why why?
In ev'ry season we ask:
Why why why why why?

Why?

Why can't everything happen the way it's supposed to?

Why can't the Dawgs we love, love us back?

Why can't X come when called, sit, stay?

Why, as Charles asked me once, on a romp with Moose at a park in New Jersey, where it seemed as if every single person in the world was walking a dog: why are all dogs cute?

The dog world has Great Danes and miniature collies, dachshunds and dingoes, and yet Charles is right, they're all cute. I didn't know what to tell him, except to say that all dogs, like all babies, seem to exude a lovable perfection that has nothing to do with their size or shape or color or breed, their length of tail or shape of ear.

Dogs never lose this universal lovability mojo, but we do. Like a baby tooth, it lets go at the root and one day it's gone. Then the fun begins. Some people fall in love with us and some people don't. Some people we can love back, some we can't. And some couples grow closer over time, while many, too many, just grow further apart.

But before that happens? When X is in its newborn, elemental form? That's the true stuff, the über-X, the X-peranto language of love that everyone can speak. The dogs in the park have it, bunnies and kittens have it, and Charles still has it, at four.

I don't know exactly when it goes. Somewhere between four and fourteen, though.

But now for some happy news (insert pulsing theme music from Caucasian News Network's evening broadcast here):

In an exclusive story, our sources report that Kat's recital was a beyond-grande, beyond-venti, ultrasuper-sized success!

And Dmitri helped! But NOT by playing the piano.

What happened, believe it or *nyet,* was this:

Jess, like the true-blue Kittenpal she is, actually did spend part of her brooding yakfest with Dmitri trying to get him to change his mind about Kat's recital. "And, boy, did he get agitated!" Jess told us afterward. " 'So what,' he said, 'another pretty girl with a violin! The record companies don't care. All they want is a horse and pony show,' but I think he meant dog and pony. Anyway, he was very bitter and said there is no music anymore, just a circus, and Kat would be better off learning to juggle than wasting time on a recital unless she came up with something nobody had done before, and what was he, just another failed Russian pianist, and so on. It went on like that for a while. But the POINT is," Jess concluded, "you HAVE come up with something that nobody has done before, and it's going to be GREAT!"

And that is how Kat finally decided to use Jacob as the accompanist for her recital. For her totally smokin', completely unprecedented, classical-violin-repertoire-meets-sitar-jammin' recital that came as near to blowing the roof off the recital hall as any performance Mr. Edgar Chorloff, legendary head of Argosy Records, could remember hearing in his fifty-year career of Making Stars.

"He told me he got his chill!" exults Kat after the recital is done and we're all clustered around the stage, worshipping her and Jacob. Mr. Chorloff practically pole-vaulted to the front of the hall to embrace Kat before the rest of the receiving line could form. "That's what Mr. Chorloff calls it. The chill he gets when he knows something is going to be big! He says we're fresh and original and that's what he's always looking for and almost never finds. He wants us in his office on Monday!" She throws her arms around Jacob's neck and hugs him, hugs him, hugs him.

Jacob, who claims to cultivate an Eastern sense of detachment, not getting too bummed about the bad things and not going too wild about the good, since everything's always changing anyway, cannot resist acting just this once like he won the Mega Millions.

"Whooooooo!" he cries, jumping up and down with Kat. *"Whooooooo!"*

I'm happy for their happiness, but inside I'm lugging around a little suitcase of sad. And Randall is giving ME the invisible treatment. My mega-apologetic e-mail (written in haste and at great length after Jess and I figured out the et sweatera snafu!) is still Status Unread, and he refuses to even make eye contact at school. He came to the recital, as befits his position as Kat's former pretend boyfriend, but sat by himself and snuck out during the applause, before I could even think of something useless and stupid to say to him.

Matthew came to the recital, too, and Trip and Deej, of course. Deej even lent Kat that knockout yellow sheath dress for the occasion. With her swingy, butter-colored hair and the creamy yellow dress, Kat looked gorgeous, like a shaft of sunlight on the stage.

And guess who else showed up? Jacob's *maman*, the illustrious Mother Thespian herself. Her *Medea* had been extended and then she had a small independent film to shoot, so she'd been in Canada filming. They wrapped yesterday and she high-tailed it back to New York, coming directly from the airport to the recital hall. Jacob is used to her being away so much, of course, but you could tell he was tickled she made it.

A good thing she did, too! Before the recital, Kat's biggest worry was how her dad would take the whole Rachmaninoff-with-a-sitar concept. Now that it's over, Mr. Arlovsky is visibly struggling to say something nice. He certainly appreciates Jacob's musicianship, as well as his excellent manners.

"But what about the composer's intentions?" he starts in, unable to resist the argument. "No, no, Katarina, don't roll your eyes! You must consider: when does creativity of interpretation stop and the destruction of centuries of musical tradition begin—"

But in that split second, as the crowd disperses and he gets his first eyeful of Jacob's mother sitting in the auditorium, Mr. Arlovsky forgets all about centuries of musical tradition and pretty much everything else.

"Excuse me! But do you know who that is?" Mr. Arlovsky exclaims, clutching his chest. "That is Elizabeth Baxter! The greatest classical actress of our time!" He turns to Kat. "What is she doing here, Katushka?"

"Well," says Kat, turning to her fellow musician. "I think Jacob should tell you."

Jacob grins, a little bashful. "Easy to explain, sir. She's my mom."

"Elizabeth Baxter is your MOTHER?" Mr. Arlovsky struggles to keep his voice low. *"Bleepsky bleeping Streepsky bleep!"* He kisses Jacob hard on both cheeks and strides over to where Mother Thespian sits with her luggage, patiently waiting for her son to gather up his accolades so they can, at long last, go home.

New Yorkers are funny about famous people. They'll strike up a conversation with an ordinary stranger at the drop of a hat but believe the truly famous are entitled to some privacy. So, though there has been much pointing and whispering from a discreet distance, Elizabeth Baxter is sitting quite alone, fanning herself with her program and looking every inch the legend of stage and screen that she is.

Mr. Arlovsky clicks his heels together and bows. "Madame," he says, in his Russian-inflected bass. "I saw your Nina in *The Seagull* many years ago, when you were on tour in St. Petersburg. It was impossible to believe that a non-Russian woman like yourself could capture, with such perfection, the beauty of this play! And in English, no less! Such a feeble language, compared to Russian! I have been your devoted follower ever since. Your Masha, Arkadina, Ranyevskaya–I have seen them all. You are–a divinity!"

"Not a bad speech, considering the feebleness of the language!" Kat whispers to me, giggling.

The greatest classical actress of our time has no doubt heard similar praise before. But she smiles with such delight you'd think she'd just opened her acceptance letter to drama school. "You are so very kind," Elizabeth Baxter says, in those famously expressive tones. "And, you are Russian?"

"Da!" says Mr. Arlovsky with pride.

The Divinity gestures for him to sit beside her. "May I ask you something?" she says irresistibly. "There is another of your countrymen here. I overheard him purchasing his ticket in the lobby, and that wonderfully attractive accent you share was unmistakable."

Mr. Arlovsky starts to blush, red as the rubies in a Fabergé egg.

"I was hoping you might know who he was," coos Elizabeth Baxter. "I'm eager to speak to him about an important professional matter."

"Who?" cries Mr. Arlovsky. "I will bring him to you immediately! Only a fool would refuse such an invitation."

"That man," she says. She indicates the back of the hall with a toss of her photogenic head.

Slouched against the back wall of the auditorium, here out of guilt, or curiosity, or just to check out the competition, is Dmitri.

Sleepy-faced, tousle-haired Dmitri, with fire and melancholy in his eyes, his curved pouty lips pink against the hungover sallowness of his skin, with bone structure like Old European royalty and really, really nice buns.

Elizabeth Baxter's voice is a soft, velvet purr, but her appraisal is cool and objective as the weekly box-office grosses in *Variety.*

"That man," she says. "That man needs a screen test."

"I love that we can share our clothes!" says Deej. "I always wanted to share my stuff with somebody, but all my girl cousins got too much—" Deej holds her hands out in front of her chest to indicate the magnitude of her cousins' ample boobs.

Kat, Jess, Deej, and I are lunching at our favorite booth at the Moonbeam. It's nice to be without Dawgs for a change. There's been so much falling into, falling out of, wanting and yearning and pining lately, I almost forgot that just hanging out with the Kittensistahs is all that.

"A *boyfriend*"–I hear my mom's voice, tickling in my brain–"a *boyfriend* is NOT the only golden road–"

But the tickle is interrupted as the Moonie delivers our cheeseburgers, flawlessly remembering that Kat's has extra onion and Jess's has Swiss instead of cheddar.

"Speaking of bosoms," says Deej, "my cousin Norma"–at which point we all hold our hands in front of our chests and crack up laughing–"just got engaged, and I need something to wear to the party. Do you have anything full-length?"

"Tons!" says Kat. "A whole closet full of recital dresses, you have to come over and look. My mom sends one every few months from Moscow. I think she thinks that's all people wear in New York. There's a really pretty white one I've never worn–I'm afraid it'll fall off when I play! Form-fitting and strapless. You would look so great in it."

"That sounds cute!" Deej agrees. "But white is too bridey for an engagement party. I don't wanna confuse the issue of who's getting married. My cousin has everyone confused enough!"

As we consume our burgers like the ferocious felines we are, Deej tells us the saga of her (insert hands in front of chest) boobalicious cousin Norma.

"Norma," she begins, "was hooked up with this guy Michael for like, two years. Michael's sweet, not too bright, but they got along, except for one thing: all the time she's complaining to him, 'Michael, your best friend Travis is no good, I don't like that brother, he is bad news, you should shake him loose.' Why she talked like that nobody knows, 'cause Travis is a brother who's got some GAME. There is NOTHING wrong with Travis, are you following me, people?"

We're following. Deej continues. "Then comes her birthday, right, and Norma lifts up her bosoms and puts her hands on her hips and says, later for this, I'm giving myself a present I've been wanting for a long time. And she says goodbye, Michael, and that very week she announces her engagement, to be married, till death do them part, to none other than—"

"Travis!" we all yell, too loud for a restaurant.

"That's right! And they're crazy in love!" says Deej. "She and Michael were all right, but her and Travis are soul mates. You have never seen anything like it."

"Definitely skip the white dress!" says Jess, chuckling and sticking a french fry in her mouth.

"Wait," I say, my every well-honed reflex of scientific curiosity on red alert. "You mean she got engaged to her soul mate after dating his best friend for two years? And treating him—the soul mate, I mean—like, well, like she didn't like him?"

"She treated him like a DOG!" Deej says, laughing. "It was painful to watch. But now she and Travis are hooked up Hollywood style, happy ending and fade out. They are together 4-evahmore."

The Moonie scribbles something on a check and slides it onto our table, where it ends up in front of me.

But I don't have to read it. I already know what it says.

Your Fifth and Final Experiment:
"The Best-Friend Switcheroo"
It's our pleasure to serve you! Please come again!

Matthew and I are in the lab, literally hopping around with excitement at the insight offered by the story of Boobalicious Norma.

But we are up against the clock. Today is Wednesday, the science fair is Monday, and Saturday I'm supposed to go to Lauraville. Before then we have charts to draw, handouts to type up, and the required oral presentation to write and rehearse, so there's hardly time for one more experiment. However:

Randall is still really, really mad at me. I don't think he's too pleased with Matthew, either.

And, Matthew, though 99 percent accepting that Jess is not interested, can't help 1 percent wondering if Jess would feel differently about his Dawgappeal if she weren't busy brooding over some Russian wolfhound.

In short, we both want one more chance to find X. Not in a chart or a graph or a hypothesis, but in a hand-holding, joke-sharing, be-my-valentining kind of real-life way. And Experiment Number Five is going to be IT!

The rules of the Best-Friend Switcheroo are simple. You scorn the person you really want and pretend to be in love with his (or her) best friend. So:

If I have to scorn Randall and pretend to be in love with his best friend, and . . .

If Matthew has to scorn Jess and pretend to be in love with her best friend, then . . .

Are you following me, people?

Matthew and I have to pretend to be in love with each other!

O, X-cellent irony! X is a trickster, all right, a mustachioed carnival barker who'll take your last nickel for one more spin of a wheel that's rigged. But that's what we're going to do. We don't have two years to wait for the Switcheroo to work its mojo, like Boobalicious Norma did, but we're hoping a single strategically planned encounter will make an impact.

One sweet, romantic episode of me and Matthew holding hands, calling each other baby darling and honey smoochums, his arm round my shoulder, my adoring eyes batting away at him for all the world to see.

But wait! Won't that be—because wasn't I—and didn't he—

Forget all that. This is going to be total fun. Because, face it, despite some tears shed by yours truly over his truly, no tighter bonds of paldom have ever been forged between our two tribes of Kitten and Dawg as those between me and Matthew. We have been (thanks for the tip, Mom!) as open with our feelings as open can get, and we have come out on the other side with a clean slate of friendship.

But how could I have been so Xed over Matthew for so long, and now, not? Believe me, I have given this a lot of thought, ever since that balmy-on-the-outside, storm-tossed-on-the-inside night on the *Betty J.*

And since the next morning, when tear-streaked me woke up in my mom's bed and told her, as best I could, how I seemed to have mucked up my entire life's chances for love in a single evening. She listened, carefully and without saying a word, while she fixed us both some breakfast (something tasty for a change, featuring generous amounts of white flour and refined sugar, so you know she was feeling sorry for me).

"No one does anything perfectly on the first try," she said, pouring maple syrup all over the sweet concoction and putting it in front of me. "Next time you'll make different mistakes. You want some hot chocolate with that?"

And, as I'm sitting there, eating and feeling my blood sugar zoom into the stratosphere, I realize the old girl is right. If Kat has to practice for hours and hours, day after day, year after year to play a single eight-minute piece of music to her own satisfaction, then isn't it possible that X needs a little practice, too? False starts, wrong choices, big mistakes, and some hurt and even a few angry words? And I know how hard it is to keep starting over, because often enough I've watched Kat suffer and swear, turn her pages back to the beginning, and try again.

Yes, practicing is hard. But that's how you get to Carnegie Hall.

"Do you know that old joke?" I say aloud to Matthew. "How do you get to Carnegie Hall?"

"Practice," murmurs Matthew, sketching something on graph paper. "Look here. The tricky part is, we need to do the Switcheroo in a place where both Randall and Jess will see us. Any ideas?"

X X X

And so, the intrepid investigators get back to work. We conceive and quickly discard various hare-brained schemes (sorry, Frosty!): a coed esoteric sleepover party at my mom's bookstore? A Kitten-and-Dawg Hacky Sack challenge match in Central Park? But how would we get Randall to come? He's so over us right now.

Once again, Deej offers the solution.

"Miss Doris says you're all invited!" she announces at the Pound the next morning, happy as can be. "She's having her Sunday salon!"

Deej explains that now and again on a Sunday afternoon, Miss Doris opens her Harlem home to friends and neighbors and music lovers everywhere for one of her legendary salons. There's food, there's punch, and most of all, there's jazz.

Matthew and I strategize like five-star generals. Jess has been dying to meet Miss Doris, so wild horses could not keep her away from this event. And we think Randall won't fail to show up for it, either. Deej is going to sing, and he came to Kat's recital, after all. Besides, who could say no to Miss Doris?

Clearly, the Sunday salon is our last, best chance to pull off the Switcheroo. Except how will I get there? A fine time to be stuck in Lauraville! And Fatherdear has been so touchy lately, the last thing he'll want to do is make an extra trip into the city to drop me off in a strange neighborhood at some wild party filled with my out-of-control, hippie-school, head-kicking friends—

But Deej just listens to my complaining and looks at me like, what's the problem? "So BRING your people!" she says. "When you get an invitation to Miss Doris's

Sunday salon, that's an INVITATION, girl! You gotta bring ALL your people! But don't bring the dog, right? Miss Doris likes to keep all her rugs nice."

Would Dad and Laura and Charles (but not Moose) be interested in coming to Miss Doris's Sunday salon?

Would they ever! "Oh, that just sounds super!" says Laura over the phone. "Should I bring some macaroni salad?"

"I'm sure that would be fine," I say, glad she can't see the look on my face. Pulling off the Switcheroo is going to be tricky enough. Pulling it off in front of my dad is another thing entirely.

I hang up the phone with a sigh, foolishly convinced that the final complication has been added to this already complicated endeavor, and, though it's all rather daunting, at least I know what I'm up against.

"A jazz salon in Harlem with all your friends and your dad and his family? What fun! Am I invited, too?" Mom asks. She's painting her toes with blue nail polish. Which is weird, because I haven't seen her paint her toes in years.

"Yes, actually," I mumble, though it had not occurred to me to actually mention this to her, since I assumed she'd rather spend Sunday afternoon anywhere else on the planet than with Dad and Laura. "Do you want to come?"

"Only if I can bring a date," Mom chirps, fanning her toes.

So Mom is coming the salon, too. With a date.

NOW the final complication has been unveiled.

X X X

Saturday morning, during the long drive to Lauraville, I weigh my two, equally horrifying conversational options. I can tell my dad that Mom is bringing a date to the salon. Or I can tell my dad about the Switcheroo.

Walk the plank or be shot at dawn? I flip my mental coin and the Switcheroo wins. Cagey me waits till he's distracted by having to drive through the toll plaza, and then, calmly, casually, I mention that Matthew and I are going to pretend to be madly in love at the salon, even though we're just friends.

"Matthew. This is the one that's not your boyfriend?" he says.

"Right. But just for tomorrow I'm going to pretend he is," I say, trying to sound like this makes sense.

"Why?" asks Dad. "Why not just let him be your boyfriend?"

Why why why why? Why is this so hard to explain? Maybe I should tell him about Randall, but seeing as how Randall was the one who gave me the black eye that freaked my dad out to begin with, I decide against it. "It's for a science project, Dad!" I say. "It has important ramifications for, you know, the future of humanity."

The look of intergalactic dubiousness on his face seems strangely familiar, but for once he cuts me some slack, says nothing, and keeps driving.

I hope I haven't blown it. I bet Brearley is still taking applications for the fall.

Matthew and I made plans to arrive at the soirée together, soul mate style, so my dad drops me off at the corner of St. Nicholas Avenue and 145th Street to wait for my faux beau while he parks the car.

It's a bustling Sunday afternoon in Harlem. Not so different from the East Village, except in the obvious ways. Women and children chattering in Spanish instead of NYU students chattering in hipsterese, hair-braiding salons instead of tattoo parlors, homeboys in homeboy outfits instead of punks in punk outfits. I hear traffic and radios playing and a million people talking at the same time, and I imagine blending all their different languages into a humungous new one that has a word for anything you'd ever want to say, and everyone could understand it. Sort of like Esperanto, but I think New Yorker is what I'd call it.

I'm mulling this over when a gleaming black Mercedes makes a slow turn round the corner of St. Nicholas Avenue. The Benz pulls over right where I'm standing, and the tinted window rolls down.

"Hey, *chiquita!* Wanna ride?" Trip's mischievous face appears. I see his dad sitting in the backseat next to him and I wave, but Mr. Mathis is on his phone.

"This is close enough, Miguel, *gracias,*" Trip tells the driver, getting out of the car. "Embarrassing, right?" he says to me, gesturing to the car. "Pops insisted on dropping me off. Bye, Daddy-o!" Trip sticks his head in the car and gives his dad a smooch.

"I'll send Miguel to come get you in a couple of hours," says Mr. Mathis, covering the phone with his hand.

"Please don't, Pops."

"Take a taxi home, promise?" says Mr. Mathis.

Trip just smiles and waves. The window slides up and the Benz pulls away. I'm glad to have this chance to brief Trip on our plan. We're going to need all the support we can get to pull off the Switcheroo.

"So listen, Trip," I say, "Matthew and I are doing our last experiment today, and we'd appreciate it if you'd just play along."

I briefly outline the parameters of the Best-Friend Switcheroo.

"A bodacious experiment!" says Trip. "Kind of like how Randall fell for you when you were all hot over Matthew."

What?

"Or like when Randall was pretending to be Kat's boyfriend and you got interested in him all of a sudden."

Wait—is that what happened?

Trip goes on. "But Randall's not coming. You know that, right?"

"He's not?" I say, dumbfounded.

"Yeah, Deej invited him and he expressed his sincerest regrets, but he had to be in Utica today for a karate tournament. He left with his sensei at like, six o'clock this morning. They won't be back till late."

But, but but—

At that point, my faux beau Matthew trots down the street, a bouquet of floppy carnations in one hand. They're for me, of course. He twirls me in his arms twice before putting me down.

"Darling!" he exclaims. "How is my gorgeous girl-friend today?"

"Matthew," I say.

"Let me kiss that precious face!" he says, plopping a wet one on my cheek.

"Matthew, he's not coming—"

"Mwah!" Matthew says, getting the other cheek. Trip's hysterical already.

"Matthew!" I yell, my precious face cradled in his hands. "Randall's not coming to the salon!"

Matthew straightens up. "He's not?"

"No, he's not," I say, wiping my damp cheek. "But it's okay. We already did the Switcheroo."

"We did?" says Matthew, confused. He hands me the flowers. "Did it work?"

Trip puts one arm around each of us. "Like a charm. Now let's go hear my lady sing."

Dad, Laura, and Charles arrive at the door of Miss Doris's building just as we do, and I make sure to lift Charles up so he can be the one to press the buzzer. My dad is confused as to who is Matthew and who is Jacob, and it takes some explaining to get him to understand that this is Trip, not Jacob, an entirely different non-Matthew teenage boy than the one he met before.

When Miss Doris answers the door, she is warm and welcoming and elegant as a crane, in a long flowing print dress and big gold hoop earrings. "Oh, MY! What a super apartment!" cries Laura, zealously praising the gleaming dark woodwork and parquet floors, the wall sconces and picture molding and stained-glass transoms above the French doors.

Laura is right. It's a gorgeous old place, and the walls are covered with dozens of framed photos. Miss Doris introduces the people in them like old friends: Duke Ellington, Charlie Parker, Dizzy Gillespie, Thelonious Monk. There's a teenage girl in many of the pictures who looks an awful lot like Deej, but unless there's a time-travel machine nearby, the tall dark-eyed beauty in the fabulous 1940s dresses and hats can only be a younger version of Miss Doris herself.

The living room has a baby grand piano at one end, prettily draped with a lacy throw. Near the back of the room is a refreshment table that holds platters of food and the biggest, fanciest cut-glass punch bowl I've ever seen. It reflects the light in the room from every angle.

"Ooh! Hawaiian Punch!" says Charles, spying the enormous, sparkling bowl of cherry-colored liquid.

"I have special punch for you, honey!" says Miss Doris. "That's grown-up punch and it'd put you right to sleep. And I don't want YOU to miss the party!" She takes Charles by the hand and leads him happily to the kitchen for a juice box.

There are quite a few people here already, including Jess and Jacob and Deej, of course, but there's one woman in particular who seems strangely familiar. She's talking animatedly with a middle-aged man by the refreshment table. Her face is flushed, her hair is up, her toenails are painted blue. Whoops, it's my mom. In lipstick, no less.

She turns around at the sound of our voices, but it's my dad who speaks first.

"Frank?" he says, in wonder. "Frank Allen?"

The middle-aged man who is my mom's date approaches my dad with his arms outstretched. "Robbie, you crazy, crazy old dog!" he says, laughing.

As Dad and Frank do the back-slapping buddy hug, I turn to my mom. "They know each other?" I ask stupidly, since obviously they do.

"Oh, yes!" says Mom, giving her long dangly earrings a shake. She looks nifty, I have to admit. "They used to be best friends, a long, long time ago. Frank and I always kept in touch, and his wife died a couple of years ago, and he's been wanting to get together for the past few months but I couldn't bring myself to— well, anyway, he's always loved jazz, so I thought he'd enjoy this."

What-EVER, Mom! My ears tuned out at "long, long time ago." Inside my brain, my warning lights are flashing, my siren is sirening, I'm careening at dangerously high speeds around corners and through red lights in a state of total emergency. Ignorant and unwitting, without any idea of the potentially life-altering consequences of her actions, Mom is doing the Best-Friend Switcheroo!

ON MY DAD!

Won't this make Dad fall in love with her again?

Can it be that that's what she wants? Does Motherdear know more about the secret workings of X than she lets on?

I fantasize for a minute: what would happen if Mom and Dad got back together? If he dumped Laura and showed up in the East Village with a fistful of daisies (Mom's favorite), asking the blue-toed Cheryl for a second chance? And what if she said yes, admitting their differences were minuscule compared to their long shared history and, most of all, the unadulterated joy they share in ME? Me, Felicia! The only thing they really have in common.

What would happen? He'd never move back to the city; he wouldn't be able to stand it now that he's been gas grilled and suburbanized. And Mom would certainly not want to give up the bookstore. So there'd be a big fight about where to live.

And then there'd be a big fight about Brearley versus the Pound. And whether to keep white bread or whole wheat in the fridge.

And poor Laura would probably starve herself to death, all alone in Lauraville, living on diet root beer and low-carb pretzels.

And Charles—

Enough. I turn off my lights and sirens, take a deep breath, and decide to simply Observe.

I watch my mom help Charles stick the little straw into his juice box without squirting juice everywhere.

I watch my dad chatting amiably with Frank, who once hung out with him in the parking lots of 7-Elevens, enjoying the Slurpee brain-freeze effect while they cranked Meatloaf up to earsplitting volume on the tape deck of my grandpa's Chevy, back in the day when Meatloaf was new and music was on tape.

I watch him and Frank, who's here as the date of my dad's ex-wife and seems to have lost just as much hair as my dad has over the last twenty-odd years, and I think— you know, it's fine.

Everything's fine the way it is.

The salon was divine. Boobalicious Norma and her soul mate Travis showed up, and they give off the same sparks that are starting to fly from Trip and Deej, except they're older and engaged and that opens up a whole other world of spark-making possibilities. Deej's mother and father were there, sweet and so proud of their talented baby. Even Shally and D'Neece stopped by for a bite to eat, rolling their eyes a bit when Miss Doris spoke to them sternly about "what you children are doing with your young lives, and there are worthier boys for two righteous girls to be spending time with than the kind you have to take the bus to Rikers to see on visiting day." But they stayed for second helpings and gave Miss Doris big hugs when they left, so I don't think they were really mad about what she said.

Mom was tense at first, as befits a woman on her first date in years, but she eventually chilled out and found her party attitude. Dad talked real estate with Deej's uncle Lester, who is raising money to fix up some of the beautiful old houses on the block without booting out the people who live in them. Laura drank too much punch, kicked off her shoes, and went on a cookie binge by the refreshment table (I've never seen her so happy). And Charles stood on one side of the stage all afternoon, dancing to the music. No matter who got up to play or sing, Charles stayed right there, shaking his little four-year old groove thang. At one point Laura tried to make him sit down but no one would let her, everyone thought he was just the cutest.

Jess, by the way, chatted at great length with Miss Doris, clapped and stomped her feet for all the performers, and paid not one bit of attention to Matthew other than the generic, hey-buddy-see-ya-in-school-tomorrow kind. I offered to try the Switcheroo on her, but Matthew declined. I can see why. He and I could have been making out naked on the stage and Jess wouldn't have batted an eye; she was too busy being ENTHUSIASTIC about the soirée.

And all afternoon, in between everyone else, Deej sang. She sang everything anybody asked her to sing. She sang gospel songs, Motown songs, Barbra Streisand songs, Aretha and Patti Labelle and Patsy Cline and Judy Garland songs. She crooned and rapped and wailed and danced the Locomotion with Charles, who started calling her Deesha.

"Now I have two sisters," Charles whooped. "Deesha and Feesha! Deesha and Feesha!"

That, by the way, was the end of being Felicia, to everyone except my mom.

I am now known to one and all as Feesha, 4-evah-more.

12

~~The Science Fair~~ My Friend Matthew

All votes have been counted and the results are in—faculty, students, parents, and four out of five dentists agree, this is the biggest and brainiest and most bodacious Manhattan Free Children's School science fair evah!

Go, Free Children! Free Children ROCK!

There are more than fifty projects, each one more edifying than the next. From where I'm sitting onstage I can see the guys in the dark suits from NASA and MIT and Microsoft scampering round like bunnies, taking copious notes and pressing their business cards into the hands of my fellow adolescent researchers.

Everybody, and I mean everybody, is here, except Randall. My mom is here, but no Randall. All the Kittens and Dawgs are here (including Trip, who seems to have whipped together a last-minute science fair project of his own), and Randall is absolutely not among them.

Even Mr. Frasconi is here! He finally made it back to New York, early this morning, just in time to be the Mister Mentor Master of ceremonies of the whole she-bang. It's been so crowded that we've only been able to wave across the gymnasium at each other. Now we're onstage in front of everybody and he's about to introduce Project Number Forty-two "The Search for X," so this isn't a great time to ask him, but I'm betting that the plump and pretty blond lady I saw him strolling around with earlier must be his Foxy Fräulein, the sweeter-than-a-jelly-donut Miss Elke Wolfgram herself.

And still there is no Randall. Attention, science fair passengers! You are now entering a Randall-free zone.

Mr. Frasconi gives me an encouraging wink before turning back to the microphone. "This next project," he says, completely ignoring the scripted introductions he's been given, "is of great personal interest to me as a poet, and as a man in love!" He beams at his Fräulein, who beams back at him from the auditorium, her cheeks aglow. "These two young scientists have fearlessly ran-sacked their own hearts, striving to know the unknow-able! What could be truer to the spirit of scientific inquiry? And what topic more timeless and universal than the mysterious workings of human affection?"

Ohmigod. I see Randall, at the far, far end of the gym. He's slipping in at this very moment through the big double doors, silent and ninja-like, invisible to all eyes except mine. Mere coincidence? I think not!

"Ladies and gentlemen," roars Mr. Frasconi, "I give

you Project Number Forty-two, 'The Search for X.' Prepare to learn . . . the Secret of Love!"

Matthew and I approach the podium.

"Before we reveal the Secret of Love," I say, my voice reverbeverbeverberating over the mike, "I want to point out that it's okay if you don't really understand what we're about to say. Some things you can't really 'get' until you go through them yourself."

At this, my mom starts cackling from the audience, which is good because it makes my nervousness go *pffft!* and disappear. I grin and wave in her direction. "Yes, Mom, I know that's what you always say to me. Gloat in triumph, because I totally admit your rightness on this ONE particular point!"

Now all the parents start laughing. Matthew gives me a sly look and takes over the mike. "The details of our experiments have been fully documented," he says. "If you stop by our table, you'll learn all about X, the mysterious factor that makes love work out."

Randall wanders over to our display, which is near the back of the gym. I mentally will him to stop and pick up one of our handouts (which have little good-luck nibbles around the edges, courtesy of Frosty).

I speak again, as Matthew and I rehearsed. "You'll see how we conducted primary source interviews to Observe and Describe the workings of X, and used experiments to test our hypotheses." I have to refer to my notes here. "These included the Romeo/Juliet Thing, Opposites Attract, Mutual Rescue, the Romantic Setting, and the Best-Friend Switcheroo."

It's kinda cool how you could hear a pin drop in the

gymnasium all of a sudden. Randall is still at our table, reading. It's now or never.

I keep going, my voice loud and clear. "All the data is presented in detail on our charts and handouts, so I won't go into it further except to say this:

"Snow melts to reveal
All that was misunderstood.
We need to talk. Please?

"If you have any questions, I'll be waiting at the back of the gym in fifteen minutes," I blurt. "And now"– (insert Imaginary Drumroll here!)–"Matthew Dwyer and I are pleased to reveal . . . the Secret of Love!"

I turn the mike over to Matthew. He looks at me strangely and clears his throat. "Ahem. The Secret of Love has two parts," he says. "An axiom and a corollary. The axiom: Love Happens."

I step forward. "The corollary: Love Happens to Everyone." Is Randall still here? I can't see him anymore; the stage lights are shining right in my eyes.

"Love Happens is a way of saying that love has its own navigational system," Matthew continues. "It starts, it stops, it takes off, and it lands, but we can't tell it where to fly. Is this good news or bad news? Look at it this way: our experiments proved that X is real." He flashes me his half-smile. We both know he sounds a lot like me right now, but that's mostly because I wrote this part. "It's like rain–it's hard to predict exactly when it's going to fall. But you definitely know when you're getting wet."

"The corollary: Love Happens to Everyone." I had

carefully planned how I was going to explain the corollary, but I am so incredibly jazzed about my own fearlessness–go, Feesha!–that I decide to improvise. "This is also known as the Meg Ryan Rule," I say, abandoning my script, Frasconi style. "See, in a movie, if Meg Ryan's in it you KNOW she will definitely have X and be madly clinching with whatever guy she wants by the end of the film."

A murmur of assent ripples through the crowd. Matthew's looking at me like I just went nuts. "I'd like to thank my mom for pointing this out to me," I go on. Not to mention the Deck of Hollywood Stars. But a science fair is not the time to start giving credit to esoteric messages from the Great Beyond, and I've been way too busy to have even thought of consulting the Oracle in a long time. Besides, Momski deserves the boost.

"Before undertaking this project, I used to think that some people have X–like Meg Ryan, or even Matthew, here," I say. There are some titters in the audience. "And that other people don't have X at all. Like me, for instance."

Matthew puts his hand on my shoulder, buddy-like, as I go on. "But our experiments have proven, beyond a doubt, that we're all capable of spewing mass quantities of X," I say. "Every single one of us is the Meg Ryan of our own love movie."

The crowd is hanging on my every syllable. "It's just that your X only really activates when it comes into contact with compatible X, at the right time and under the right circumstances, and"–I shield my eyes against the lights as I finish–"you have to make sure you take your blinders off first."

I give Matthew the wrap-it-up signal, and we end our presentation by inviting members of the audience to come to the microphone and tell their stories of X. How it happened, how it didn't happen, how it almost happened and unhappened and happened again. (The audience participation angle was Matthew's idea, by the way, something about qualitative data versus quantitative, but who cares, I think it's a snazzy touch!)

A long line forms at the microphone, but I don't need to listen. There's only one X-story I'm interested in right now, and I'm going to know the ending in exactly fifteen—make that lucky THIRTEEN—minutes.

Twelve minutes and forty-five seconds later, I'm in the back of the gym, and Randall's walking right toward me.

"Hey," he says.

"Hey," I say.

"Nice presentation," he says. "Looks like you're a hit."

We look up at the stage, where Mr. Frasconi is hogging the mike, holding hands with his Foxy Fräulein and telling their X-story in Teutonic Technicolor detail. Miss Wolfgram is blushing two little red circles on her cheeks, like a Dresden china doll.

"You guys should definitely win," Randall says. He's holding one of our handout sheets. "Your project is awesome. Somebody was chewing on it, though."

"It was Frosty," I said. "For luck." I know I should play it cool, but I can't bear the suspense. "Did you read that?" I ask. "The Best-Friend Switcheroo part? And the Romantic Setting? They're all about you."

"Yup," he says. He stares at his sneakers.

"I'm sorry for the mix-up, Randall," I say. "I still want to go out with you. Really."

"You do?" Randall says. It's not so much a question as an expression of disbelief.

"Yeah," I say. "If you want to."

"I feel bad about getting so upset with you," he says. "On the boat. That was such a weird night. That Romantic Setting mojo, it's really something."

"It is," I say.

"I apologize for that," he says. "I'm sorry."

"Apology accepted," I say. "But I like that you're open with your feelings, Randall." I take his hand, or he takes mine, I can't tell which. "I like that about you."

"But I should have trusted you more, too," he says. "I should have, you know. Listened."

Now we're making as much eye contact as four eyes can make. "I wish we could start over," Randall jokes. "Maybe we could go beat up some bad guys together. That seemed to work last time."

I know he's kidding, but boy, have I learned my lesson! When you're trying too hard to make X happen, the trying only gets in the way.

"Forget that!" I say. "Why don't we just go out for a burger or something? Hang out? See what happens."

"Sounds good," Randall says. "This afternoon I'm training at the dojo. How's tomorrow? A burger at the Moonbeam after school? Maybe a walk in the park? The farmer's market is open at Union Square. They sell really good apple cider donuts."

"Perfect," I say. "Donuts are perfect."

X X X

I have to admit that Matthew and I did not win anything at the science fair. But guess who took first place?

Harold Johnston Mathis the Third, that's who! Project Number Seventeen, "A Nonalcoholic Champagne Distillery," was the surprise hit of the day. Seems that Trip has found a way to brew nonalcoholic champagne that is virtually indistinguishable from Veuve Clicquot.

To demonstrate this, Trip had to bring in a few cases of his dad's best vintage champagne (marked "For Teachers Only," of course). The judging faculty tasted Trip's brew carefully but found it necessary to keep returning to the actual Veuve to maintain a basis of comparison. By the time they had to choose a winner for the science fair, the judges were unanimous in their selection of Project Number Seventeen and very, very happy.

"The worst thing about getting sober is the lack of champagne," Trip explains, handing out cups of the bogus bubbly as all the Kittens and Dawgs gather round to congratulate him. "So I decided to take matters into my own hands."

"Is this what you served on the *Betty J*?" I ask him, guzzling the tasty drink with abandon now that I know it's only seltzer plus some mystery ingredients, including, apparently, pulverized Almond Joy bars and a sprinkling of burnt toast.

"Of course," he says, handing cups to Deej and Jess.

"So why did Dmitri get drunk?" I ask. Surely the Romantic Setting couldn't be THAT powerful.

Trip laughs and pours refills for everyone. "The mind is an amazing thing," he says. "You just have to *believe*."

X X X

As the crowd in the gymnasium disperses, my mom makes some lame joke about "staying too long at the fair" and says she'll see me at home for dinner. But the real reason she's booking out is that she's meeting Frank at Starbucks for coffee. I heard her making plans on the phone this morning.

Go forth and X-iply, O blue-toed Cheryl!

Speaking of phone calls, my dad, who missed the science fair completely because he's on his way to Singapore on one of his ultraglam business trips, actually remembered to call to say good luck even though it's already tomorrow where he is, or yesterday, I forget which way the time travel works. He hasn't mentioned Brearley since the salon. Maybe he realized my life is not such a mess after all, once he got a closer look at it. My life, I mean. My room, still a mess.

So Matthew and I, a little disappointed about not winning but superhappy for Trip and proud of our achievements nonetheless, get two take-out chais from the Moonbeam and go for a quiet, celebratory stroll in Madison Square Park.

We take possession of our usual bench, near the playground. Everything's turning green in the park.

"Cheers," Matthew says. "We did it."

We sit and sip our chais. A pair of pigeons is squabbling over some old corn chips. Science is hard work, that's for sure. I'm looking forward to getting back to my poetry.

A fresh slew of pigeons join the pair in front of us. They peck, strut, take to the air briefly, and settle down again in fresh configurations, black and white and gray and orange and piebald. It's amazing how they all seem to know what to do and when to do it, without any talking or planning or instruction, without being given any data at all.

I watch the birds, and the new green grass. Nature poems would be fun, I think. Animals, plants. Weather. I'll have to discuss this with Mr. Frasconi tomorrow.

Tomorrow!

"Hey," I say. "I've got a date with Randall tomorrow."

"Cool," says Matthew. "Don't take any guff from the Randinator! Feesha deserves the best!"

"Thanks," I giggle. "I'll remember that."

I wonder if I should ask him about whether he likes anyone new, now that his crush on Jess is *histoire*. But he seems to be thinking about something else.

The little kids are starting to arrive at the playground. Matthew and I watch them take over the benches, race to the swings, scramble up the slide. I bet some of them have newly folded cootie catchers in the pockets of their windbreakers, predicting with absolute certainty which ones of them will marry which other ones.

Pick a color! *O-R-A-N-G-E,* Matthew! You picked Matthew! Ewwwwwwww!

"Paste breath!" a little boy yells, throwing a fistful of grass into a girl's hair. "You have paste breath!" He runs, and with an expression of ferocious clarity, the girl chases him round and round the playground, getting closer with each lap.

"I think he likes her," Matthew and I say, at exactly the same time, like we planned it but of course we didn't.

And we crack up laughing.

Yet another reason why I'm friends with Matthew Dwyer.

maryrose wood grew up on Long Island and moved to New York City at age seventeen. She currently lives in Manhattan with her two children, who are both remarkable even by New York standards.

This is her first novel, but Maryrose also writes for the theater and film. Her work as a lyricist and librettist has won prestigious awards. These are nice but are often presented at award ceremonies, for which it is very, very difficult to choose an outfit.

Maryrose has a cat but secretly prefers dogs, and does not ride her bike as often as she would like. She strives to live with the appropriate mixture of coolness and whimsy and suspects this may in fact be the golden road to happiness. She will let you know how it turns out.